1828

DAVID PRESTON

ISBN:
Hardcover 979-8-9905622-5-7
Paperback 979-8-9905622-4-0
eBook 979-8-9905622-3-3

Azalea City Publishing, LLC
Mobile, AL 36693
www.azaleacitypublishing.com
Cover design: Artillery Design Company Ltd
https://www.artillerydesign.co.uk/

DEDICATION

To My Brother, for helping me develop the alternative universe
this book series hopes to create.

To Sharon

ACKNOWLEDGEMENTS

Thank you to Brian Lambrecht for diligently reviewing this book and being overly critical of it. Your input has made for a vastly superior book.

Prologue

December 22, 1828

Andrew Jackson sat by the bedside of his ailing wife, Rachel. The dimly lit room was melancholy as the evening sun cast long shadows through the lace curtains. Rachel's breathing was labored, and her once bright eyes had grown dim. He held her frail hand in his, feeling her warmth slowly fading.

"Andrew," she whispered, her voice barely audible, "I fear my time has come."

Tears welled up in his eyes, but he managed to give a weak smile. "Don't speak of such things, my love. You'll get through this, just as you always have."

Rachel's hand trembled, and she clutched his hand tightly. "I wish I could, but I've known for some time. The doctors can't save me, and I don't want to suffer any longer."

Andrew's heart ached. He leaned closer, his eyes locking onto hers. "We've faced many hardships together, Rachel. I can't imagine a life without you by my side."

She smiled, though the effort pained her. "Our love will endure, my dear. Promise me, you'll always remember me and keep my memory alive."

Tears streamed down his cheeks. "I promise, Rachel. You'll forever be in my heart. I'll cherish the moments we've shared."

Rachel's breathing became even shallower. She whispered, "Tell them... to take care of you." Her grip on his hand weakened.

"I will, my love," he whispered, his voice choked with grief.

In those ultimate moments, they exchanged a loving gaze, a silent acknowledgment of their deep and enduring bond. And as the day dipped below the horizon, Rachel Jackson took her last breath, leaving Andrew with a profound emptiness in his heart.

The room fell into silence, broken only by the soft silence of Andrew Jackson, a man who had faced countless battles and challenges, but none that could compare to the loss of his beloved Rachel.

***

After Rachel's last breath, Andrew kissed her forehead one final time and reluctantly released her hand. He stood up, his legs trembling, and quietly exited the dimly lit bedroom, closing the door behind him. He was met with the soft glow of candlelight in the hallway, and the Hermitage's grandeur suddenly felt oppressive.

As he descended the creaking wooden hallway, memories of their life flooded his mind. He reached the parlor, where friends and family had gathered, their faces marked by worry and anticipation. Their eyes turned toward him as he entered.

Andrew cleared his throat, his voice carrying the weight of grief. "My dear friends and family," he began, "it is with a heavy heart that I must share the news. Rachel has departed this world, and she is at peace."

Gasps and sobs filled the room, and Andrew's own eyes welled with tears. He continued, "She passed surrounded by love, with her hand in mine. Her suffering is over, and her spirit will forever live on in our hearts."

Rachel's niece, Emily, clutched her handkerchief to her face, tears streaming down her cheeks. "Oh, Uncle Andrew, she was a true angel."

Andrew nodded, his voice quivering. "Indeed, she was, and she always will be." He looked around at the somber faces in the room, feeling a profound sense of gratitude for those who had gathered to support him.

"Please," he implored, "let us remember the joy and love she brought into our lives. She wouldn't want us to mourn for long. We will celebrate her life, her kindness, and her enduring spirit."

One by one, family and friends approached him, offering their condolences and sharing their memories of Rachel. Amid their sorrow, a sense of unity and love emerged, reminding Andrew that, even in their grief, there was strength in their bonds.

The night passed in a mixture of sorrow and reflection, as stories of Rachel's warmth, laughter, and kindness filled the air. Jackson, a man who had faced battles on the field of war and in the political arena, now faced the greatest battle of all—saying goodbye to the love of his life. And in the days and years to come, he would carry her memory with him, ensuring that Rachel's legacy would never be forgotten.

With the weight of grief heavy upon him, Jackson retreated to his study. The room was adorned with countless books, maps, and the trappings of a lifetime dedicated to service and leadership. However, today it was a sanctuary for his sorrow.

He closed the door behind him, shutting out the whispers and condolences that echoed through the home. It was starting to feel more like a solitary prison by the moment. In this private chamber, he sank into the well-worn armchair by the window, the soft light of the setting sun casting a warm glow across the room.

As he grieved for Rachel, he found solace in the memories they had created together. He recalled their laughter, their shared dreams, and the moments of tenderness that had sustained him through the storms of life. Tears streamed down his face as he clutched a locket containing a lock of Rachel's hair, a cherished memento that she had given him long ago.

But amid the grief, a profound sense of duty welled up within him. He had always been a man of strong convictions, and the nation's turmoil weighed heavily on his mind. He knew that secession, the notion that the Southern states might break away from the Union, was gaining momentum. It was a dire solution.

Jackson took a deep breath, gathered his strength, and turned to his writing desk. He felt compelled to pray, seeking guidance and wisdom in this critical moment. Bowing his head, he whispered words of comfort, seeking solace in faith, and asking for clarity in the decisions he was about to make.

As he finished his prayer, he reached for a quill and inkwell. With careful deliberation, he began to compose a letter that would be published in Democratic newspapers across the country. It was a plea for sacrifice, a call for Americans to remember the principles upon which the nation had been founded. But it was also a warning, a stern message that secession, while a grave step, might be the only way to preserve the principles of liberty that he held almost as dear as his wife.

The words flowed from his pen as he drafted a letter that would not only express his grief for Rachel but also his fervent belief in the righteousness of his cause. He knew that by publishing this letter, he would be taking a stand that would define his legacy.

When the last words were written, he sealed the letter with wax and took a moment to reflect on the gravity of the path he had chosen. With Rachel's memory as his guiding light, he was ready to send this missive to the world, in the hope that it would resonate with those who shared his ideals and those who would be called upon to make tough decisions in the turbulent years ahead.

***

My Fellow Citizens,

I pen these words with a heavy heart, for they carry the weight of a nation's turmoil and my own profound sorrow. It is with great reluctance that I find myself compelled to address you on a matter of such gravity. I must speak of secession, a topic that should fill any patriot with apprehension and sorrow, yet a course of action that I believe has become a dire necessity.

Our young Republic stands at a crossroads, torn by strife and plagued by political corruption. The very foundations upon which our great nation was built are under siege, and the spirit of liberty, so ardently defended by our forefathers, is being eroded.

In the year 1824, I, Andrew Jackson, stood as a candidate for the office of the President of the United States. In a contest marked by the voices of the people, I received the majority of both the popular vote and the electoral college. It should have been a resounding affirmation of our democratic principles, the voice of the people manifesting in their choice for leadership.

However, the circumstances of that election have left a cloud of suspicion and doubt that I can no longer ignore. John Quincy Adams, it is widely believed, secured the presidency through political maneuvering and a "corrupt bargain." This event, a stain on our democracy, cast a shadow of doubt over the legitimacy of the government.

I have wrestled with this issue in my heart, pondered it in my study, and prayed for guidance. The question that looms before us is this: Can we, as patriots, continue to pledge allegiance to a government that has strayed so far from the principles of liberty, fairness, and representation?

My friends, it is with great sadness that I have come to the conclusion that we may have no choice but to initiate secession from the Union. This is not a call to arms or a desire for division; it is a desperate plea to preserve the principles upon which our nation was founded.

It is my fervent hope that this letter serves as a wake-up call, not only to those who share my convictions but to all Americans who believe in the ideals of freedom, justice, and the right to self-determination. The course of action I propose is drastic, but the circumstances in Washington demand nothing less.

We must reflect on our history, on the sacrifices of our forefathers, and on the aspirations that have defined our great nation. We must remember that, in the face of injustice and corruption, the spirit of America has always been one of courage and determination.

Let us, as free citizens, engage in peaceful discourse, debate, and prayer to determine the course of our future. Our collective decision should be grounded in the spirit of democracy, fairness, and love of country.

May we find a path forward in secession, which preserves the principles upon which our Republic was built. And may we honor the memory of those who have sacrificed for our liberty and the principles that have guided us since the birth of our great nation.

With respect and a heavy heart,

Andrew Jackson

Chapter 1

The Campaign Begins

January 2, 1828

In the private dining room of the Executive Mansion, President John Quincy Adams sat down to have breakfast with his wife, Louisa Catherine. The room was adorned with fine China and elegant silverware, starkly contrasting to the festive decorations that still adorned the White House from the previous New Year's celebrations.

John was a man of great intellect, known for his sharp wit and quick temper. As he sat at the head of the table, his demeanor was characteristically serious, his piercing eyes focused on a stack of documents that had been placed beside his plate.

Louisa, his wife of many years, watched him with a mixture of concern and affection. "John, can we not put aside these papers for just a moment and enjoy our breakfast in peace? It's a new year, and I had hoped for a more festive start to the day."

He sighed and looked up at her, a faint smile breaking through his solemn expression. "My dearest Louisa, you know I cannot easily set aside my responsibilities, even for a morning as special as this. There are matters of great import that require my attention."

As they began to partake in their morning meal, Adams could not help but reflect on his political challenges. The election of 1828 loomed, and the bitter taste of past controversies still lingered. He had not forgotten the acrimony surrounding his election in 1824, nor the accusations of a "corrupt bargain" with Henry Clay.

Louisa Catherine reached across the table, her hand gently covering his. "John, I understand the burdens of your office and the sacrifices you make for our nation. But on this day, I wish to see you at ease. The country is watching, and they need to see their President as a man who can find joy amidst the duties of his station."

He met her gaze with affection, his stern facade giving way to a moment of vulnerability. "You are right, my dear. I carry the nation's weight on my shoulders, but I must remember the importance of balance, of finding moments of joy and celebration."

With the morning sun cast a warm glow through the windows of the dining room, the President and his wife continued their breakfast, determined to find a brief respite from the challenges that awaited them in the political arena. It was a moment of unity, a shared commitment to their country, and a reminder that they could find solace and connection in their enduring love even amid their duties.

The atmosphere was one of rare tranquility as the President and his wife enjoyed the last few bites of their breakfast. However, that moment was short-lived, as the door to the dining room swung open, and the President's Chief of Staff, Richard Wilkinson, entered with an air of brisk efficiency. He was a man of military bearing, and his presence commanded immediate attention. His arrival disrupted the quietude, but it was a reminder of the relentless pace of the presidency.

"Mr. President, Mrs. Adams," Wilkinson said with a nod, "I trust you had a pleasant morning. I apologize for the interruption, but the business of the day awaits."

John Quincy sighed and set down his teacup, exchanging a resigned glance with Louisa. "Very well, Richard. What's on the agenda for today?"

Wilkinson approached the table and placed a stack of official documents before the President. "We have a series of meetings scheduled, including discussions with key members of Congress on the national infrastructure bill. Additionally, several diplomatic matters require your attention, particularly the ongoing negotiations with the British."

Adams frowned, realizing his hopes for a peaceful and reflective morning had been dashed. "Very well, Richard. I will attend to these matters shortly."

Louisa Catherine, ever the diplomat herself, chimed in, "My dear, remember to find moments of respite even amid your busy day. It will make you a more effective leader."

The Chief of Staff, knowing the delicate balance of managing the President's time, acknowledged her wisdom with a nod. "Of course, Mrs. Adams. I will do my best to ensure the President has time for duty and rejuvenation."

A sense of purpose in his movements, President Adams rose from the breakfast table, his expression resolute. "Thank you, Richard. Let us begin the work of the day. There is much to be done, and I will face it with the dedication that our great nation deserves."

As the President and his Chief of Staff made their way out of the dining room, Louisa watched them go, a mix of pride and concern in her eyes. It was a reminder that the weight of leadership never truly lifted. They moved down the elegant corridor of the executive mansion toward the President's office. The

President was deep in thought, mentally preparing for the day's meetings and negotiations.

Wilkinson, always a step ahead, laid out the schedule for the day as they walked. "We'll start with the infrastructure bill discussions, then meet with the British envoy to continue the negotiations. After that, you have a conference with the Secretary of State and the Secretary of the Treasury."

Adams nodded, his mind racing through the issues that needed to be addressed. "Very well, Richard. Let's make the most of this day."

As they entered the President's office, with its stately wooden furniture and the stars and stripes hanging on the wall, there was a sense of gravity in the air. It was a space where important decisions were made and charted.

But their discussion was soon interrupted, as the door to the office swung open, and a man of authority entered. He was James Thornton, the Campaign

Manager for President Adams's reelection bid, and he carried an air of urgency.

"Mr. President, Chief of Staff," Thornton began without preamble, "I apologize for the intrusion, but we have an urgent matter to discuss."

President Adams exchanged a glance with Wilkinson, concern etching across his face. "What's happened, James? Is it the campaign?"

Thornton nodded gravely. "Yes, sir. We've received troubling reports of political opposition and increasing tension in the country. Some factions are actively working against your reelection, and we must address this immediately."

As they gathered around the President's desk, Adams leaned forward, his brow furrowing with concern. "Tell me more, James. What do we know?"

Thornton proceeded to detail the reports and information they had received. There were allegations of smear campaigns. Accusations that Adams had promised the Secretary of State's position to Henry Clay in exchange for a favorable vote in the House in 1824. Four years of political maneuvering by Andrew Jackson since the 1824 election, and heightened partisan divisions fermented by Martin Van Buren, the wiley Senator from New York that threatened the stability of the nation. It was clear that the upcoming election would be more contentious than ever.

Adams listened intently, absorbing the gravity of the situation. "We must be prepared for a challenging campaign, James," he responded vigorously. "Our principles, our vision for this nation, will guide us. We will not waver."

Wilkinson chimed in, "We'll need to strategize, both in terms of policy and messaging. We cannot afford to underestimate our opponents."

The President, though burdened by the concerns of the day, retained a sense of resolve. "We face difficult times, but we have faced adversity before. Our commitment to our principles will guide us."

With that, they began to discuss campaign strategies, recognizing that the business of governance and the path to reelection were deeply intertwined. The challenges were great, but they were determined to navigate them, even if that meant that they would have to pull out all of the political chicanery they've ever thought of before and some they haven't yet.

With the Chief of Staff departing to oversee the day's meetings and negotiations, President John Quincy Adams and his campaign manager found themselves alone in the office. Their conversation hung heavy in the room as they faced the daunting task of running a successful reelection campaign.

Adams, with a furrowed brow, turned his attention to Thornton. "James, I appreciate your candidness. The reports about the opposition and the current political climate are concerning. Tell me, what are our chances of success, given the popularity of Andrew Jackson?"

Thornton hesitated, knowing the gravity of the President's question. "Sir, the polls are not in our favor. Jackson's widespread appeal, especially in the South and West, makes this an uphill battle. But we must remember that polls are snapshots in time. Public opinion can shift rapidly, and with a strong campaign, we can sway voters in our direction."

Adams nodded "We've faced adversity before, James, and we have always stood by our principles. The well-being of this nation is at the heart of our campaign, and we must communicate that effectively. If we can't, then we'll have to come up with a plan to keep the presidency. Jackson cannot be given the powers that this office holds, he is too dangerous to be trusted with them."

Thornton leaned forward, his voice carrying a sense of determination. "Agreed, Mr. President. We'll need a well-thought-out strategy, focusing on policy, the economy, and our commitment to the future of this country. Your leadership has always been guided by principles, and we need to convey that to the American people. We also need to make sure that the American people understand that Jackson would be disastrous for our government and our democracy."

The President's eyes fixed on the flag hanging on the wall, a symbol of the nation's ideals. "We must ensure the continuation of the democratic experiment that our fathers embarked upon. The division in our country, as evidenced by Jackson's popularity, highlights the urgency of our mission."

Thornton nodded. "We have assembled a dedicated team to craft a compelling message, and utilize every tool at our disposal, including the press and campaign events, to reach the American people."

Adams exhaled, his mind racing with thoughts of the challenges ahead. "We must demonstrate that we can lead, unite the nation, and that our vision for America's future is worth believing in. James, I will rely on your expertise to ensure we run a campaign that reflects our values and resonates with the people. I will also trust that you will do everything to ensure Jackson never sets foot in this office."

The campaign manager's resolve matched that of the President. "We will work tirelessly, Mr. President, to convey your vision and principles. It will be a challenging endeavor, but we will not fail, whatever the cost."

As they concluded their meeting, President Adams and James Thornton knew they faced an arduous campaign fraught with obstacles. But in the echoes of their resolute conversation, there was a shared commitment to the ideals that had guided their lives and the nation's future. The office, once again a place of contemplation and decision-making, was now the heart of their campaign, where they would forge a path forward in the face of adversity.

After Thornton left the President's office, John Quincy Adams took a moment to collect his thoughts. He walked to his imposing wooden desk and sank into his chair, a venerable piece of furniture that had seen countless hours of deliberation and decision-making.

As he gazed at the stars and stripes hanging on the wall, Adams contemplated the challenges ahead in his reelection campaign. The specter of Andrew Jackson's popularity loomed large, casting a shadow on his prospects. But he was not one to back down from a fight, no matter how dirty it had to get.

With a sigh, Adams reached for a pile of newspapers that had accumulated on his desk. The daily headlines, his connection to the pulse of the nation, awaited his attention. He needed to stay informed, to understand the shifting tides of American politics.

One headline caught his eye: "Jackson and the Democrats Ramp Up Election Efforts." The President's brow furrowed as he unfolded the newspaper and began to read the article. The words were a stark reminder of the challenges he faced.

The article detailed Andrew Jackson's campaign efforts, painting a vivid picture of the General's popularity and the fervor of his supporters. Adams knew that Jackson had a charismatic appeal that extended to the common man, a quality he had always loathed.

"Jackson's campaign's barnstorming tour of the South has drawn large crowds and fervent supporters," the article read. "His populist message resonates with voters, promising a change from the political elite."

As Adams continued to read, he was struck by the contrast between his approach to governance and Jackson's charismatic appeal. He had always been a man of principles, dedicated to serving the nation, but he understood that these qualities might not be enough in the face of Jackson's populist charm.

The President's mind churned with thoughts as he considered his campaign strategy. He knew he needed to communicate his vision for the nation effectively and connect with the American people on a personal level, or at least communicate to the American people that Jackson must be stopped because of his danger to the country.

Closing the newspaper, he sat back in his chair, his expression a mix of determination and reflection. The campaign ahead would be grueling, and the odds were stacked against him, but he would not back down from a challenge.

As he turned his gaze to the American flag on the wall, Adams reminded himself of the principles that had always guided his life and political career. The nation was at a crossroads, and his commitment to his future was unwavering, regardless of what was best for the country.

With a sense of purpose, he set the newspaper aside and returned to his work, ready to face the turbulent waters of the upcoming election with the steadfast resolve that had defined his presidency.

Chapter 2

A Storm is Brewing

January 8, 1828

The morning dawned crisp and clear in Nashville, Tennessee. Andrew Jackson had spent the previous evening at the Nashville Inn, having arrived from his beloved plantation anticipating an important day. As the sun's first rays pierced through the curtains of his room, he stirred awake, his mind already focused on the tasks at hand.

He swung his legs over the side of the bed, the wooden floor cool beneath his feet. Jackson was a man of action, a military hero turned statesman, and the call of duty had brought him to Nashville on this significant anniversary.

Though the memory of the battle outside New Orleans, a defining moment in his career, was etched in his mind, Jackson knew that the day held another historic milestone. He was to address a joint assembly of the Tennessee Legislature, accepting their nomination for the presidency of the United States.

After donning his attire, Jackson went to the window that overlooked the city. Nashville, a place he had called home for many years, was a thriving center of political activity, and it was here that his journey to the highest office in the land would begin.

As he descended the grand staircase of the inn, the staff and guests recognized him and greeted him with nods of respect and warm smiles. The atmosphere in the inn was charged with anticipation for the day's events and the inn's dining area was a focal point of anticipation.

Seated at a reserved table, Jackson was joined by his wife, Rachel, his campaign manager, Francis Williamson, and the Speaker of the Tennessee State House of Representatives, Samuel Powell. It was a gathering of individuals who played pivotal roles in Jackson's political journey.

Breakfast was served, with hot coffee and an assortment of biscuits, fruit, and eggs. Rachel, a graceful and steadfast presence, sat beside her husband. The love and support between them were palpable.

Williamson set the tone of the conversation. "General, today is a momentous day. The eyes of the nation are upon us."

Jackson nodded, his eyes reflecting his unwavering determination. "Indeed, Francis. It's a day that sets the course for our campaign, for the people's voice to be heard."

Samuel Powell, the Speaker, leaned in, his voice carrying the weight of the occasion. "General Jackson, the Tennessee Legislature stands united behind your nomination. The people of this state believe in your leadership."

Rachel, always a source of strength and wisdom, added her perspective. "Andrew, you've always been a man of principle. Your dedication to the common man and the cause of democracy is unwavering."

Jackson, known for his directness and commitment to his vision, responded with gratitude. "I'll carry the principles of battle into this campaign, a campaign that aims to ensure everyone's voice is heard, and that corruption and elitism have no place in our government."

The conversation flowed as they discussed the upcoming speech, the themes that would be emphasized, and the importance of uniting the nation under the banner of Jacksonian Democracy.

Ever the strategist, Williamson outlined the key points that should be addressed. "General, we need to underscore the themes of democracy, accountability, and a government that serves the people. We'll resonate with the American people by making them a central part of our campaign."

Jackson's eyes fixed on Rachel as he responded. "Our campaign is about the future of this nation, and I promise to carry the people's aspirations with me."

As Andrew Jackson, accompanied by his wife Rachel and campaign manager stepped out of the Nashville Inn on that crisp clear Tennessee morning, they were met by a scene of bustling excitement. The streets were alive with well-wishers and throngs of people who had come to see the man they believed would lead the nation.

The journey to the state capitol building, where Jackson was to address a joint session of the legislature and accept their presidential nomination, was not a straightforward one. At every step, they were stopped by enthusiastic crowds, their faces filled with hope and anticipation.

The first encounter was with a group of children, their faces beaming with admiration. "General Jackson, we want to give you a big hug!" one of them exclaimed. Jackson knelt, his towering presence softened by the interaction, and embraced the warmth that only children can exude.

Rachel, always the embodiment of grace, greeted the people with a smile. "Thank you for your support. We're honored to have your encouragement."

Williamson, keenly aware of the schedule, gently urged them forward. "We appreciate your enthusiasm, but the General has an important speech to deliver."

As they continued down the street, the crowd grew larger and more fervent. It was clear that Jackson's popularity was not limited to the state legislature; it extended to the people of Nashville and beyond.

One man, his face etched with determination, stepped forward. "General Jackson, we believe in you! You're the leader for whom we've been waiting!"

Jackson, his eyes reflecting his spirit, nodded. "Thank you. I promise to stand for the principles of democracy and a government that serves the people."

Well-wishers of all ages and economic backgrounds lined the streets, shaking hands, offering words of encouragement, and voicing their support for the campaign. Each encounter left an indelible impression on Jackson and his companions, a reminder of what was at stake.

As they neared the state capitol building, the crowd reached its peak. The cheers and applause were deafening, and the air was filled with banners and signs displaying slogans of support for Jackson.

Rachel, standing by her husband's side, leaned in and whispered, "Andrew, look at these people. They believe in you."

Jackson, a man of few words but deep conviction, responded, "I believe in them too. We'll carry their hopes with us."

Arriving at the Tennessee State Capitol building in Nashville, Jackson, accompanied by Rachel and his campaign manager, was greeted by a sense of grandeur and history. The neoclassical architecture of the Capitol, with its towering columns and imposing facade, bore witness to the democratic processes that would unfold within.

As they entered the building, their footsteps echoed in the marble hallways. Jackson, a man who had lived through the birth of the nation and fought for its ideals, moved with a dignified presence. Rachel, a source of unwavering support, walked by his side, her grace and poise a complement to her husband's charisma.

Williamson, the campaign manager, navigated the logistics, ensuring that things were proceeding smoothly. He leaned in to speak to Jackson. "General, we have a few minutes before your address. This is a momentous occasion, and the legislators and fellow citizens await your words."

Jackson, his eyes scanning the grandeur of the Capitol, nodded. "I understand the importance of this moment. Let's proceed."

They began their journey down the hallways, stopping to greet legislators and fellow citizens who had gathered for the occasion. Jackson's presence commanded respect, and the assembled were eager to extend their support.

One legislator, a man of distinguished years, approached Jackson with a hearty handshake. "General Jackson, your vision for a government that serves the people has resonated with us. We believe you can lead this nation forward."

Rachel, always gracious in her interactions, added, "Thank you for your belief in Andrew's principles. We're honored to have your support."

Williamson, aware of the time constraints, encouraged them to continue. "General, we must make our way to the governor's office."

As they progressed down the hallways, the Capitol building seemed to come alive with the enthusiasm of the well-wishers. Each interaction reaffirmed the significance of the day and the weight of the responsibility on Jackson's shoulders.

A group of citizens, diverse in age and background, formed a spontaneous cheer. "Jackson for President! Jackson for President!" The chant reverberated through the corridors.

Jackson, known for his steadfast spirit, acknowledged their support. "I stand for the people and their aspirations. Together, we can bring about a new era in American politics."

Rachel held his arm as they approached the governor's office. "Andrew, the people believe in you. The path ahead may be challenging, but we're united in our commitment."

Williamson led them to the governor's office, where preparations were underway for Jackson's address. The room was filled with legislators, supporters, and members of the press, all eager to hear the words of the man who had become a symbol of democracy.

As Jackson stepped into the governor's private office, the room fell silent, and the Capitol building seemed to hold its breath. It was a moment of historical importance, and the address to follow would set the tone for the campaign and a vision of government by the people, for the people.

The Tennessee State Capitol was to become the setting for a momentous chapter in American history, a testament to the enduring power of democracy and the voice of the common man.

In the grandeur of the governor's office, Governor William Carroll sat behind his desk, a man of poise and authority. The room was adorned with portraits of Tennessee's historical figures, each symbolizing the state's journey through its formative years.

Andrew Jackson, flanked by Francis Williamson, entered the office. Jackson was poised to address a joint session of the legislature and accept their nomination for the presidency of the United States. His presence, a blend of strength and determination, was a testament to his vision for a new era in American politics.

Governor Carroll, rising from his seat, extended his hand to Jackson. "General Jackson, it's an honor to receive you as we gather here on an auspicious occasion."

Jackson, a man who had risen through the ranks of the military and now sought to ascend to the nation's highest office, met the governor's handshake with a firm grip. "Governor Carroll, I'm deeply grateful for your hospitality and support of the legislature."

Carroll, a man of political acumen who had long served Tennessee, understood the significance. "Indeed, General. Your vision for a government that serves the common man and upholds the principles of democracy has resonated with the people of this state. We believe you are the leader we need."

Williamson, who had been orchestrating the campaign's strategy, interjected. "General, we should be heading to the Assembly Hall soon. The legislators and crowds are awaiting your address."

Governor Carroll, mindful of the schedule, agreed. "You're right, Mr. Williamson. General Jackson, the people have lofty expectations of your leadership. We look to you for a vision that will guide this nation."

Jackson responded with a sense of purpose. "I understand the weight of this moment, and I promise to carry the aspirations of the American people forward."

With a final exchange of words and a nod of mutual understanding, they made their way to the assembly hall, where the joint session of the legislature was gathered.

As Andrew Jackson stepped to the podium, the room filled with legislators, supporters, and members of the press, all eager to hear his words. The governor's office had been a place of conversation and understanding, and now it was time for Jackson's vision to resonate through the Capitol building and reach the hearts of those gathered. A vision that would set the course for a transformative campaign and a new era in American politics.

The grandeur of the House of Representatives chamber was a sight to behold. The room was adorned with rich mahogany furnishings, high vaulted ceilings, and ornate chandeliers that bathed the space in warm, golden light. Portraits of the state's historical luminaries gazed down from the walls, bearing witness to the momentous occasion that was about to unfold.

As the time for Andrew Jackson's address to the joint session of the legislature drew near, the chamber buzzed with anticipation. Legislators, dignitaries, and well-wishers had filled the space, each seat occupied, the air charged with the significance of the day.

The door of the chamber swung open, and there, escorted by Governor William Carroll, stood Andrew Jackson. His presence was commanding, a testament to his military heroism. As he entered the chamber, the hush of expectancy fell over the room.

The Sergeant-at-Arms of the House of Representatives, a figure of ceremonial authority, announced in a booming voice, "Ladies and gentlemen, I present to you General Andrew Jackson!"

The announcement was met with an eruption of applause and a standing ovation. The legislators rose from their seats, and spectators in the galleries added their voices to the acclaim. It was a resounding show of support for a man who embodied the aspirations of the people.

As Jackson made his way through the aisle, the crowd parted before him, eager to get a glimpse of the man who had come to symbolize a new era in American politics. His stride was steady, his eyes filled with determination.

The Speaker of the House of Representatives, standing at the podium, extended his hand to Jackson. "General Jackson, it's an honor to have you with us today."

Jackson, a man who had fought battles on both military and political fronts, shook the Speaker's hand with a firm grip. "Thank you, Mr. Speaker. I'm deeply honored to be here."

As the applause continued, the Lieutenant Governor also stepped forward to greet Jackson. The moment was marked by solemnity and respect. Jackson, the symbol of a growing political movement, recognized the importance of this meeting of legislators.

With a final handshake, Jackson ascended the podium where he would address the joint session. The chamber fell into a hushed expectation, a moment of historical significance. Jackson's presence was not merely symbolic; it represented a vision of government by the people.

He stood before the gathered assembly, the eyes of legislators, supporters, and the people of Tennessee fixed upon him. The room was filled with the anticipation of the words that would shape the course of the campaign, a campaign that aimed to transform

American politics and ensure that the voice of the common man was heard.

In the chamber, Andrew Jackson prepared to speak, a figure whose actions and words would resonate through the nation.

Jackson stood at the podium, his eyes scanning the assembly of legislators, dignitaries, and well-wishers gathered for this momentous occasion. The room, bathed in the soft glow of the chandeliers, was the very essence of American democracy.

"Mr. Speaker, Mr. Lt. Governor, honorable members of the Tennessee Legislature, and fellow citizens," Jackson began, his voice a resolute and unwavering force that filled the chamber. "I stand before you today with a deep sense of responsibility, for the people of this great state have placed their trust in me. I accept with humility your nomination for the presidency of the United States."

The chamber was filled with rapt attention and ruckus applause and cheering, the anticipation tangible as

Jackson continued. "Fifteen years ago, I stood on the battlefield of New Orleans, defending our nation against foreign aggression. Today, I stand on a different kind of battlefield, one that requires the defense of our democratic principles, the will of the people, and the common man's rights."

He paused, his eyes meeting the gaze of those in the chamber. "The battle ahead is not one of musket and cannon, but one of ideas and vision. It's a battle for the very soul of our nation, a battle that will determine whether our government truly serves the people it represents."

The applause in the chamber was thunderous, a testament to the resonance of Jackson's words. He raised his hand to quell the ovation, his presence one of unwavering conviction.

"Today, we face a government plagued by corruption, where the elite and the privileged hold sway. We face a political system that favors the few over the many. But this is not the vision our Founding Fathers had for this nation. It is not the vision I have."

Jackson's words echoed through the room, carrying the spirit of democracy, a government that will respond to the will of the people. "I promise you that my campaign, my presidency, will stand for a government that serves the common man. It will stand for a government that upholds the principles of democracy, a government where the voice of the people is heard and respected."

As he spoke, Jackson's vision for the nation unfolded, emphasizing accountability, transparency, and a commitment to the common man. He spoke of a government that would end political corruption and embrace the ideals of a strong and united nation.

The room was filled with fervent applause as Jackson concluded his address. "I accept your nomination, not as an honor bestowed upon me, but as a solemn responsibility. I will carry your trust with me into this campaign and, if the American people choose, into the highest office of this land."

As he stepped away from the podium, the chamber remained abuzz with the resonance of Jackson's words. The members of the Tennessee Legislature and the well-wishers who had gathered understood the significance of this moment, a moment that marked the beginning of a campaign and a vision for a new era in American politics.

In the House of Representatives chamber Andrew Jackson had accepted the nomination with a promise, a promise to stand for democracy and a government that truly served the American people. The journey to the presidency of the United States had begun, and with it, the aspirations of a nation eager for a new era of leadership.

Chapter 3

A Party is Born

January 21st, 1828

On this crisp morning, a stagecoach rumbled into the courtyard of the Nashville Inn, drawing the attention of the inn's staff and guests. The city of Nashville was alive with activity, but this arrival was not any other. The stagecoach bore a distinguished passenger: Martin Van Buren, the prominent political figure, who had journeyed to Tennessee to meet with influential Democrats.

As the stagecoach came to a halt, the inn's manager, a stout and welcoming man, approached the carriage with an outstretched hand. "Welcome to the Nashville Inn, Sen. Van Buren! We're honored to have you with us."

Van Buren, a man known for his fashionable attire, stepped down from the stagecoach, his dark coat and impeccable grooming contrasting with the rustic surroundings. He flashed a polite smile and took the inn manager's hand. "Thank you for your kind welcome. It's good to be in Nashville again."

With the help of an attendant, he gathered his belongings, including a leather satchel that contained documents and letters pertinent to his mission. The inn's courtyard was abuzz with activity, guests bustling about, horses tethered to posts, and the aroma of freshly cooked breakfast filling the air.

As Van Buren made his way through the inn's entrance, a few patrons recognized him, exchanging knowing nods and whispered words of admiration. He acknowledged them with a gracious nod and proceeded to the inn's reception area.

The innkeeper's wife, a genial woman with a warm smile, greeted him, "Sen. Van Buren, we've prepared a comfortable room for your stay. You'll find it to be your home away from home during your visit."

Van Buren thanked her and, with his key in hand, was escorted to his quarters, where he could relax and prepare for his important meetings in the days ahead.

The purpose of his visit to Nashville was no secret. As a prominent figure in the Democratic Party, he was here to rally support and forge alliances in the lead-up to the 1828 presidential election. The popularity of Andrew Jackson, a fellow Democrat, had not gone unnoticed, and Van Buren was determined to play a pivotal role in ensuring Jackson's victory.

Motivated by a sense of excitement and trepidation, Martin Van Buren settled into the Nashville Inn, a place where political ambitions and strategies would be discussed and where the fate of the nation's highest office hung in the balance.

The dining was bustling with activity, as guests and travelers gathered to partake in the morning meal. The clinking of silverware and the murmur of conversation filled the room, creating a lively atmosphere. At the center of this commotion, a table was reserved for a gathering of significant importance.

Seated at the table were two familiar figures: Andrew Jackson and his campaign manager. Their presence had already drawn the attention of those in the dining area, and whispers of excitement rippled through the room.

As breakfast was being served, Martin Van Buren entered the dining area. The Senator cut a distinguished figure, his polished demeanor standing out in the rustic inn. His keen political instincts and strategic thinking had earned him respect among his peers.

As Van Buren approached the table where Jackson and Francis Williamson sat, the campaign manager rose from his chair, extending a warm greeting. "Senator, it's an honor to see you here. Please, join us."

Van Buren offered a polite smile and took his seat between Jackson and Williamson. "Thank you, Francis. It's good to be here." He turned his attention to Jackson, his face lighting up with an air of camaraderie. "General Jackson, it's always a pleasure to see you, especially here in Tennessee."

Jackson nodded appreciatively. "Martin, you're a welcome guest in my home state. We have much to discuss in the days ahead."

The trio delved into their breakfast, exchanging pleasantries and anecdotes about the political climate. It was clear that the 1828 election loomed large in their minds, and the popularity of Andrew Jackson, the leading Democratic candidate, was a central theme.

Van Buren, ever the astute strategist, broached the subject. "General, your appeal to the people is undeniable. We've seen the crowds that gather at rallies and the enthusiasm of your supporters. We must harness this momentum to victory in the upcoming election."

Jackson leaned forward; his eyes filled with determination. "Martin, I trust your judgment. We need a clear message, a vision for this nation that resonates with the common man. The people have placed their trust in us, and we must not fail them."

Williamson chimed in, "We've outlined a rigorous campaign schedule, with strategic stops throughout the country. We must connect with voters on a personal level."

Van Buren nodded, his mind already racing with ideas. "We must not underestimate our opponents, gentlemen. The road to victory will be fraught with challenges, but our shared commitment to the principles of democracy and liberty will guide us."

As breakfast progressed, the trio discussed campaign strategies, key policy points, and the importance of presenting a united front to the American people. The Nashville Inn had become a focal point for their discussions, a space where the fate of the nation's highest office was being shaped.

With the sun casting a warm glow through the inn's windows, Van Buren, Jackson, and Williamson were united in their resolve. They understood the magnitude of the task before them and were determined to secure a victory that would shape the future of the United States.

Martin Van Buren had spent the last four years in the United States Senate methodically working to obstruct President John Quincy Adams' agenda. From the moment he took his seat in the Senate, Van Buren had been a thorn in Adams' side, employing a combination of calculated maneuvers and strategic abstentions.

Van Buren's opposition to Adams' administration was rooted in his belief that the President was corrupt. He had voiced these concerns on multiple occasions, convinced that the government needed a change from what he perceived as a culture of political elitism.

One of Van Buren's most effective tactics was his strategic abstention from voting on key issues. He was well aware that the Vice President, John C. Calhoun, held the tie-breaking vote in the Senate. By abstaining from votes, Van Buren would often force Calhoun to cast the deciding vote, thereby creating a visible rift within the administration's ranks.

This subtle yet potent maneuvering disrupted the unity of Adams' team, as Calhoun, a former ally, was increasingly caught between loyalty to the President and alignment with Van Buren's anti-administration camp. The Vice President's apprehension about breaking with the administration became a matter of public scrutiny, deepening the internal divisions.

In the Senate chamber, Van Buren was an expert in parliamentary procedure, using his influence and strategic alliances with other senators to stall or thwart Adams' legislative efforts. He raised objections, introduced amendments, and called for extended debates, all to slow the administration's progress.

Van Buren's power in the Senate extended beyond his parliamentary tactics. He used his eloquence and political acumen to rally like-minded senators around his vision for a new direction in American politics. He found willing allies in those who shared his suspicions of corruption in the Adams administration.

His greatest triumph was in obstructing Adams' ambitious infrastructure bill, a central piece of the President's agenda. Van Buren and his allies framed the bill as a wasteful government project that would benefit the elite at the expense of the common man. With his skilled oratory and persuasive arguments, he successfully delayed the bill's passage and derailed one of Adams' signature initiatives.

Throughout these four years, Martin Van Buren remained steadfast in his belief that the government needed to shift away from what he saw as a culture of corruption. He saw himself as a champion of the American people, advocating for a more transparent and accountable government. His efforts in the Senate, whether through abstentions, strategic maneuvering, or passionate speeches, were all aimed at promoting his vision for a better future for the nation.

In doing so, Van Buren set the stage for the upcoming presidential election, where his alignment with Andrew Jackson and the growing movement of Jacksonian Democracy would usher in a new era in American politics. His opposition to Adams' administration had been successful in thwarting the

President's agenda and laying the groundwork for the seismic shifts that were about to reshape the nation's political landscape.

Over breakfast at the Nashville Inn, Martin Van Buren, Andrew Jackson, and Francis Williamson found themselves immersed in a new topic of conversation, shifting from Van Buren's Senate tactics to the critical matter of who would be the best running mate for Jackson in the upcoming presidential election. The choice of a vice-presidential candidate was a matter of utmost importance, one that could shape the course of the campaign.

Van Buren sipped his coffee as he leaned forward, his tone thoughtful and determined. "Gentlemen, we must consider the qualities and background of our running mate carefully. The message we send to the American people needs to be unequivocal. Uniting the country under Andrew's leadership is our priority."

Williamson, always pragmatic and detail-oriented, listened intently. "You're right, Martin. We need a running mate who complements General Jackson's strengths and broadens our appeal to voters."

Jackson, a man of few words but resolute conviction, nodded in agreement. "Indeed, it's a decision we must make carefully. The running mate must stand for the same principles that guide us."

Van Buren wasted no time in putting forth his candidate. "I believe John Calhoun would be an excellent choice. He hails from South Carolina, a region we must secure. But more than that, his experience and background in the National Republican Party brings elements of Adams' supporters into our camp."

The campaign manager raised an eyebrow, seeking clarification. "You're suggesting that Calhoun's inclusion on the ticket would help bring in elements of Adams' party?"

Van Buren nodded. "Precisely. He's been a prominent figure in Adams' administration, and his support for internal improvements aligns with Adams' policies. If we choose Calhoun, we can appeal to those who may have grown disenchanted with Adams but are not necessarily aligned with the National Democrats."

Jackson, known for his skepticism of Calhoun, took a moment to consider the proposal. "It's an interesting idea, Martin. Calhoun's inclusion might unify the nation, but we must be certain of his loyalty to our cause."

Van Buren leaned in, his tone earnest. "General, I've had discussions with Calhoun, and I believe he is committed to advancing the principles of democracy and the common man's interests. We can have assurances of his loyalty."

As the conversation continued, the trio explored the idea of Calhoun as Jackson's potential running mate, acknowledging the complexities and risks involved. The decision was not to be taken lightly, for it would shape the direction of their campaign and the future of the nation.

In that bustling dining area of the Nashville Inn, amid the clinking of cutlery and the hum of morning conversations, the fate of their campaign began to take shape. The choice of a running mate was a pivotal decision that would influence the hearts and minds of the American people as they headed into the tumultuous presidential election of 1828.

As breakfast continued, Van Buren, Jackson, and Williamson delved deeper into the discussion of their upcoming presidential campaign. The conversation had evolved from choosing a running mate to the broader idea of uniting the anti-Adams forces under a single banner, which would lead to a new political party.

Van Buren, his mind focused on the bigger picture, spoke with conviction. "Gentlemen, it's clear that the time has come for a new political movement, one that unites all those who stand against the perceived corruption and elitism of the Adams administration."

Williamson, ever the pragmatic campaign manager, inquired, "Martin, are you suggesting that we form a new political party?"

Van Buren nodded, his gaze steady. "Yes, a party that embodies the principles of democracy, the will of the people, and a commitment to a more transparent and accountable government. We need a unifying force that brings together the disparate groups who share these ideals."

Jackson, a man of action, leaned forward, his eyes reflecting his commitment to the cause. "I've long believed in the power of the people. If we can create a party that stands for these principles, I will lead it."

Williamson, ever the realist, considered the logistical challenges. "We'll need a name, a platform, and a strategy for the campaign. It's a monumental undertaking."

Van Buren, not one to shy away from a challenge, responded, "That's true, but it's a challenge worth embracing. As for a name, let's choose one that reflects the ideals of our movement. How about 'The Democratic Party'? It sends a clear message of inclusivity and commitment to the principles of democracy."

Jackson agreed with a nod. "The Democratic Party it is. We need to build a platform that emphasizes the common man's interests, a government that serves the people, and a commitment to states' rights."

The trio continued to outline the key tenets of their new party, discussing the importance of widespread suffrage, a reduction in government power, and an end to political elitism. The Nashville Inn, a witness to their fervent discussion, was now the birthplace of a new political movement.

In that moment, the seeds of the Democratic Party had been sown, and a vision had taken shape. The upcoming presidential election of 1828 would not only be a battle for the nation's highest office but a defining moment in American politics. The inn's dining area buzzed with the excitement of their ambitious undertaking as they concluded their breakfast, they were united by their unwavering commitment to the principles of democracy and a vision for a more inclusive and accountable government.

62

The stage was set, and a movement had been born, one that would reshape the political landscape of the United States and leave a lasting impact on the nation's history.

Chapter 4

Fake News

February 11th, 1828

In the morning the sun cast a warm glow over the Hermitage, Andrew Jackson's plantation nestled in the heart of Tennessee. The grandeur of the estate, with its white columns and sprawling landscape, was a testament to Jackson's success, as a military leader and a statesman.

In the dining room, a hearty breakfast had been prepared. Jackson, his silvery hair and rugged demeanor belying his age, sat at the head of the table. Rachel radiated warmth and grace as she took her seat beside him. The couple had seen their share of challenges, both on the battlefield and in the political arena.

"Andrew," Rachel began, her voice carrying the gentle cadence of a woman who had been through much with her husband, "there's much to be done today.

The estate needs attention, and we have guests to entertain."

Jackson nodded in agreement. "You're right, Rachel. We'll tend to the estate's affairs, and I'll meet with some of our supporters later."

Williamson sat at the other end of the table, a sense of purpose in his demeanor. "General, the campaign is picking up momentum. We have events to plan, and speeches to prepare. The people believe in your vision."

As they continued their discussion about the day's agenda, the room was filled with the aroma of freshly brewed coffee, sizzling bacon, and biscuits hot from the oven. The Hermitage was the setting for this pivotal moment.

Once breakfast concluded, Jackson reached for the newspaper, The Daily National Journal. As he perused the headlines, his brow furrowed at a particular article. "Rachel, listen to this," he said, his voice tinged with anger. "It says, 'Slave trader running for President.'"

Rachel leaned in to read the article, her expression mirroring her husband's apprehension. "This is a troubling development, Andrew. We knew the campaign would be challenging, but these lies add another layer to it."

Williamson, always focused on strategy, considered the implications. "We'll need to address this head-on, General."

Jackson nodded; the weight of the moment evident in his gaze. "You're right, Francis. We'll need to get the papers supporting us to run articles denouncing these lies as political slander and treachery planted by Adams' people to distract from his corruption and ineffectiveness."

They embarked on this new task of responding to this attack. The newspaper headline was a reminder that the journey to the presidency was not without obstacles, and Jackson's commitment to a government that truly represented the people would be tested at every turn.

***

Allegations Surface Regarding Andrew Jackson's Past Involvement in Slave Trading

In an astonishing revelation that has sent shockwaves through the political landscape, new allegations have emerged regarding the early life of General Andrew Jackson. According to undisclosed sources, Jackson, renowned for his military prowess and populist appeal, may have been involved in the despicable practice of slave trading during his formative years.

The allegations surfaced in recent weeks and have stirred controversy and raised questions about Jackson's character and moral standing. While details remain scarce, reports suggest that Jackson, before his ascent to prominence in the political arena, may have engaged in transactions related to the buying and selling of enslaved individuals.

If substantiated, these claims could tarnish Jackson's legacy and cast a shadow over his campaign. Despite his reputation as a champion of the common man and a defender of American democracy, the specter of involvement in such reprehensible activities threatens to undermine public trust and confidence in his leadership.

Critics have seized upon these allegations as evidence of Jackson's purported hypocrisy, citing the stark contrast between his professed values and the alleged exploitation of human lives for financial gain. Calls for transparency and accountability have intensified, with demands for a thorough investigation into Jackson's past and a reckoning with the truth.

Supporters of Jackson, however, have vehemently dismissed the allegations as baseless smears orchestrated by political adversaries intent on tarnishing his reputation. They argue that Jackson's record of service to the nation, including his heroic exploits on the battlefield and his unwavering commitment to the American people, stands as a testament to his character and integrity.

As the nation grapples with these startling revelations, the specter of Andrew Jackson's alleged involvement in slave trading looms large, casting a pall over the impending election. The American people are left to reckon with the complex legacy of a leader whose past actions continue to reverberate through the annals of history.

*****

American Royalty Thinks He's Entitled to Presidency

In a charged political climate, John Quincy Adams, the incumbent President, finds himself at the center of controversy today. Critics are pointing to his lineage as the son of the second President of the United States, John Adams, to suggest that he feels entitled to the highest office in the land.

The question being asked by many is, does a famous last name equate to a claim for the presidency?

John Quincy Adams entered the White House in 1824 with lofty expectations. However, his presidency has been marked by a fiercely divided nation, accusations of corruption, and questionable policies, which have led some to question his suitability for a second term.

Andrew Jackson, the celebrated war hero and statesman, has emerged as a formidable opponent. His campaign has galvanized those who believe that the presidency should not be an entitlement but a responsibility to the American people.

Jackson's supporters argue that the time has come for a leader who stands for the common man, a leader who will challenge the entrenched interests in Washington, and a leader who understands that true democracy demands more than just a famous name.

As the presidential campaign intensifies, the choice between these two candidates becomes a choice between tradition and change, aristocracy and democracy, and the entitlement of the few versus the will of the many.

***

*Controversial Allegations Surrounding Rachel Jackson's
Marital Status Cast Shadow on Campaign*

In a startling twist of events, the legitimacy of the marriage between General Andrew Jackson and his beloved wife Rachel has been called into question, plunging the nation into a maelstrom of controversy and uncertainty. Recent revelations suggest that Rachel Jackson may have been entangled in a legal and moral quandary before her union with Jackson, raising doubts about the validity of their marriage.

According to sources close to the matter, it has come to light that Rachel Jackson was previously married to another man before entering into matrimony with Jackson. These reports allege that Rachel's prior marriage had not been properly dissolved or annulled, rendering her subsequent marriage to Jackson null and void in the eyes of the law.

If substantiated, these claims could have far-reaching implications for the Jacksons and the legitimacy of their union. Questions abound regarding the legality of their marriage and the ramifications for Jackson's presidential campaign, which is set to continue in the coming months.

Critics of the Jacksons have seized upon these allegations as evidence of deceit and moral turpitude, painting the couple as duplicitous and unworthy of the nation's highest office. They argue that the Jacksons' apparent disregard for the sanctity of marriage and the rule of law undermines their moral authority and calls into question their fitness to lead.

Supporters of the Jacksons, however, have dismissed the allegations as baseless attacks aimed at besmirching the reputation of a beloved leader and his devoted wife. They contend that the Jacksons' enduring love and commitment to each other transcend any legal technicalities or bureaucratic hurdles, reaffirming their belief in the strength of their union.

As the nation grapples with these troubling revelations, the specter of illegitimacy hangs over the impending candidacy of Andrew Jackson, casting a shadow over the nation's political landscape. With the conclusion of Jackson's campaign drawing near, the American people are left to ponder the implications of these revelations and their potential impact on the nation's future.

***

Jackson slammed the newspaper down on the breakfast table. "That scallywag!" He exclaimed "He is attacking my family now! These lies will not go unpunished!" He balled his hand into a fist and slammed it into the table in front of him. As Racheal walked into the room, he turned to her and said, "If I was younger and this wasn't a national race, I would shoot Adams dead in the street for spreading these lies about you." "They aren't lies," Racheal responded with a dejected look on her face as she looked down at the letter in her hand. "Lewis sent me this letter saying that our divorce wasn't final when you and I married and that he was suing me for a divorce now and you for marital interference." Andrew's demeanor instantly changed, and he got up, embraced his wife and said, "I will fix this darling, don't worry, everything will be okay."

***

Adams Struck a Corrupt Bargain to Get the Presidency

A dark cloud of suspicion hangs over the presidency of John Quincy Adams, as claims of a corrupt bargain that secured him the highest office in the land resurface. The question on everyone's mind is, did Adams compromise the principles of democracy to ascend to the presidency?

It is no secret that in the hotly contested election of 1824, no candidate secured the majority of electoral votes. The election was sent to the House of Representatives to decide, where Henry Clay, then Speaker of the House, held a position of profound influence.

Critics have long alleged that a nefarious deal was struck behind closed doors between Adams and Clay. The accusation is that Clay, having dropped out of the presidential race, threw his support behind Adams in exchange for the position of Secretary of State. This move allowed Adams to secure the presidency despite not winning the popular vote.

Jacksonian Democrats, led by Andrew Jackson, have vehemently criticized this supposed "corrupt bargain." They argue that such political maneuvering goes against the principles of democracy and is a blatant disregard for the will of the American people.

Jackson's campaign has seized upon these allegations, presenting the 1824 election as an example of political elites manipulating the system to maintain their power. They contend that the people deserve a president who will rise to power through the people's voice, not through backroom deals.

As the 1828 presidential campaign heats up, the charge of a corrupt bargain against John Quincy Adams becomes a central issue. It is a stark reminder of the fierce competition between Adams and Jackson, both of whom promise to bring a new vision to the nation.

Chapter 5

An Enduring Love

March 1, 1828

The soft light of dawn filtered through the curtains of the Hermitage, casting a warm glow across the room. Andrew Jackson stirred in bed, his thoughts already churning with the day's momentous events. Beside him, Rachel Jackson lay still, her breathing steady, but the tension in her face was evident. Today was the day they would right a wrong that had cast a shadow over their lives.

Andrew turned to Rachel, gently brushing a stray lock of hair from her forehead. "Rachel, my love, it's time to get up," he said softly. "We have a big day ahead of us."

Rachel opened her eyes slowly, blinking against the light. "Good morning, Andrew," she replied with a faint smile. "I suppose we do."

Andrew sat up, the weight of the situation pressing heavily on his shoulders. They had recently discovered that Rachel's divorce from her first husband, Lewis Robards, had not been finalized at the time of their marriage. This revelation had brought scandal and heartache, but today they would set things right by remarrying properly.

"I'll go check on the preparations," Andrew said, swinging his legs over the side of the bed. "You take your time getting ready. We want this to be a beautiful day for you."

Rachel nodded, her eyes following him as he stood up. "Thank you, Andrew. I just hope this will finally put all the gossip to rest."

Andrew leaned down and kissed her forehead. "It will, Rachel. And it doesn't change how I feel about you.

We've been through so much together, and this is just another step in our journey."

As Andrew left the room, Rachel took a deep breath and got out of bed. She moved to the window, looking out over the sprawling grounds of the Hermitage. The sun was rising, casting a golden hue over the fields and trees. It was a new day, a day of new beginnings.

In the kitchen, the staff was bustling with activity, preparing breakfast and making sure everything was perfect for the wedding later that day. Andrew entered, his presence commanding but calm.

"Good morning, everyone," he greeted. "How are the preparations coming along?"

The head cook, Idamae Thompson, looked up from her work with a smile. "Good morning, General

Jackson. Everything is going along nicely. We'll have breakfast ready in just a few minutes."

"Thank you, Idamae," Andrew replied. "I appreciate all your hard work."

He turned to see one of his aides approaching. "Eaton, have you made sure the minister has everything he needs for the ceremony?"

"Yes, sir," Eaton replied. "The Reverend is preparing now, and the garden is being decorated as we speak."

"Excellent," Andrew said, nodding. "And the guests?"

"They've been informed of the change in plans and are expected to arrive shortly," Eaton confirmed.

"Very good," Andrew said, a sense of relief washing over him. "Let's make sure everything goes smoothly."

Upstairs, Rachel was getting dressed with the help of her maid, Sarah. She wore a simple but elegant dress, one that reflected her quiet strength and grace.

"How do I look, Sarah?" Rachel asked, turning to her maid.

"Beautiful, Mrs. Jackson," Sarah replied with a smile. "Mr. Jackson is a very lucky man."

Rachel smiled, though her eyes were tinged with sadness. "Thank you, Sarah. I just want this to be over, so we can move on with our lives."

"It will be, ma'am," Sarah said reassuringly. "And everyone will see how much you and Mr. Jackson love each other."

Rachel nodded, taking comfort in Sarah's words. "You're right. This is just another chapter in our story."

When Rachel finally joined Andrew downstairs, the dining room was filled with the aroma of freshly baked bread, eggs, and bacon. The table was set beautifully, and Andrew was waiting for her with a smile.

"You look radiant, Rachel," he said, pulling out a chair for her.

"Thank you, Andrew," she replied, taking her seat. "And thank you for making all of this possible."

Andrew sat down beside her, taking her hand in his. "It's the least I could do. Today is about us, about our love and our future."

As they ate breakfast, their conversation was filled with memories of their life together and hopes for the future. Despite the cloud that had hung over them, their bond was unbreakable.

Later that morning, as the guests arrived and the final preparations were made, Andrew and Rachel stood together, ready to face the next chapter of their lives.

The breakfast table at the Hermitage had been cleared, and the staff was busy with the finishing touches for the afternoon ceremony. Andrew stood at the front door, greeting the first of the arriving guests, while Rachel Jackson made sure everything was perfect inside.

Andrew's old friend, John Overton, approached the steps with a broad smile. "Andrew! It's good to see you."

"John!" Andrew exclaimed, shaking his hand firmly. "I'm glad you could make it."

"You think I'd miss this for the world?" John replied, clapping Andrew on the back. "Rachel must be thrilled to have this day finally come."

"She is," Andrew said, a proud smile spreading across his face. "It's been a long road, but we're here."

Inside the garden, Rachel was directing the placement of flowers and overseeing the arrangement of the chairs. Her friend, Mrs. Donelson, approached with a warm smile.

"Rachel, everything looks beautiful," Mrs. Donelson said. "You've done a wonderful job."

"Thank you," Rachel replied, her eyes scanning the garden to ensure every detail was perfect. "I just want this day to be special."

"It will be," Mrs. Donelson assured her. "Everyone can see the love you and Andrew share. That's what matters most."

As more guests arrived, the Hermitage buzzed with excitement. Friends, family, and notable figures from Andrew's political life mingled, their conversations filled with anticipation and joy.

"General Jackson!" called out Senator Sam Houston as he arrived. "A fine day for a wedding, don't you think?"

"Indeed, it is, Sam," Andrew responded, shaking his hand. "I'm glad to see you here."

"Wouldn't miss it," Houston said, looking around. "You've got quite the turnout."

Andrew chuckled. "Rachel has a way of bringing people together."

Shortly thereafter Martin Van Buren joined the gathering. "General, it's an honor to be here," he said, his voice sincere.

"Martin, thank you for coming," Andrew said, embracing his hand firmly. "Your support means a lot to us."

Van Buren nodded. "This is a day for celebration, and it's important to be here for both of you."

As the guests settled, the atmosphere was one of warmth and camaraderie.

After the ceremony, the celebration continued with a grand reception at the Hermitage. Guests mingled, enjoying the food and drink, and sharing in the couple's happiness.

Rachel, surrounded by friends, laughed as they reminisced about old times. "Do you remember when we first moved to the Hermitage?" she asked Mrs. Donelson. "It was such a different place back then."

"I do," Mrs. Donelson replied, smiling. "You've turned it into a beautiful home."

Andrew, meanwhile, was in deep conversation with John Overton and Sam Houston. "It's been quite a journey," he said. "But I wouldn't change a thing."

Houston raised his glass. "To Andrew and Rachel," he toasted. "May your love continue to grow and inspire us all."

"To Andrew and Rachel," the guests echoed, raising their glasses.

As the sun set over the Hermitage, the celebration continued late into the evening. Andrew and Rachel, hand in hand, watched as their friends and family danced and laughed, their hearts full of gratitude and love.

In the quiet moments after the festivities had ended, Andrew and Rachel stood together on the porch, looking out over their beloved home.

"We did it," Rachel said softly. "We're finally married properly."

Andrew pulled her close. "We did, my love. And nothing can ever come between us again."

Rachel smiled, resting her head on his shoulder. "I love you, Andrew."

"I love you too, Rachel," he replied, kissing her forehead. "Now and forever."

And with that, they turned and went inside, ready to face whatever the future might hold, together.

***

The Hermitage flower garden was a place of serenity and beauty. It was Rachel's favorite spot on the plantation. It was here that she and Andrew had decided to renew their vows, surrounded by the vibrant colors and fragrant blooms that Rachel so lovingly tended to.

The guests were seated, their eyes filled with anticipation as Andrew and Rachel stood beneath an arch adorned with Rachel's favorite flowers. The Reverend stood before them, a gentle smile on his face as he began the ceremony.

"Friends and family," the Reverend began, his voice warm and welcoming. "We are gathered here today to witness the union of Andrew and Rachel Jackson. Their love and commitment to each other have endured through every challenge, and today, we celebrate their renewed vows."

Andrew turned to Rachel, taking her hands in his. His voice was steady but filled with emotion. "Rachel, from the moment I first saw you, I knew you were the one I wanted to spend my life with. Through all the trials we have faced, my love for you has only grown stronger. I vow to stand by your side, to support you, and to love you with all my heart, for as long as we both shall live."

Rachel's eyes glistened with tears as she listened to Andrew's words. When it was her turn, she took a deep breath, her voice trembling with emotion. "Andrew, you have been my rock, my confidant, and my greatest love. Your strength and your kindness have carried us through the darkest times. I vow to be your partner, your friend, and your loving wife, for all the days of our lives."

The Reverend smiled, his eyes reflecting the emotion of the moment. "By the power vested in me, I now pronounce you husband and wife. Andrew, you may kiss your bride."

Andrew and Rachel kissed to the applause and cheers of their friends and family. As they turned to face their guests, the joy on their faces was unmistakable. The guests rose to their feet, clapping and cheering for the happy couple.

Among the guests, Martin Van Buren approached, his eyes shining with happiness. "General, Rachel, congratulations. This is a day long in the making, and I am honored to be here."

"Thank you, Martin," Andrew said, shaking his hand. "Your friendship and support mean the world to us."

Rachel smiled, taking Martin's hand in hers. "Yes, thank you, Martin. We are so grateful for your presence today."

As the guests mingled, sharing in the couple's happiness, the atmosphere was one of warmth and camaraderie. The celebration continued with a grand reception, where friends and family gathered to enjoy food, drink, and the joyous occasion.

The reception after the wedding ceremony was set up in the expansive backyard and back porch of the Hermitage. Tables were adorned with fresh flowers and elegant settings, while the bright rays of sunlight created a warm and festive atmosphere. The sound of laughter and music filled the air as guests mingled and celebrated.

Inside the house, Rachel was surrounded by friends, laughing and reminiscing about old times. "Do you remember when we first moved to the Hermitage?" she asked Mrs. Donelson. "It was such a different place back then."

"I do," Mrs. Donelson replied, smiling. "You've turned it into a beautiful home."

Meanwhile, Andrew was deep in conversation with John Overton and Sam Houston. "It's been quite a journey," he said. "But I wouldn't change a thing."

Houston raised his glass. "To Andrew and Rachel," he toasted. "May your love continue to grow and inspire us all."

"To Andrew and Rachel," the guests echoed, raising their glasses.

Andrew Jr., Andrew Jackson Hutchings, Theodore, and Lyncoya stood proudly beside their parents, receiving guests and offering their congratulations.

Andrew Jr., the eldest, was the first to speak. "Father, Mother, this is a day we will all cherish. Your love and commitment to each other are an inspiration to us all."

Rachel beamed, embracing her son. "Thank you, Andrew. Your support means everything to us."

Hutchings, standing next to his brother, added, "We've seen you both go through so much, and yet, your love has never wavered. It's a testament to the strength of your bond."

Andrew Jackson clapped Hutchings on the shoulder. "Thank you, son. Your words mean a great deal to us."

Theodore, with a broad smile, chimed in, "I've always admired the way you two look at each other, even after all these years. It's something truly special."

Rachel laughed softly; her eyes misty with emotion. "Oh, Theodore, you always know how to make me smile."

Finally, Lyncoya, the youngest, stepped forward. His voice was soft but sincere. "Father, Mother, I am grateful to be a part of this family. Your love has given me a home and a place to belong."

Andrew knelt down to embrace Lyncoya. "We are blessed to have you, son. Your presence has brought so much joy to our lives."

As the family stood together, they were surrounded by friends and loved ones who shared in their joy. The backyard was filled with laughter and conversation, as guests enjoyed the delicious food and drink that had been prepared for the occasion.

John Overton approached the family, raising a glass in a toast. "To Andrew and Rachel, and to their wonderful children. May your love continue to grow, and your family remain strong and united."

"To Andrew and Rachel," the guests echoed, raising their glasses in celebration.

The evening was filled with heartfelt speeches, music, and dancing. As the night wore on, the Jackson children took center stage, sharing stories and memories of their parents that had the guests laughing and applauding.

Andrew Jr. recounted a humorous story about his father's stubborn determination during a particularly challenging campaign. "Father never backed down from a challenge," he said, grinning. "And that's something he's passed on to all of us."

Hutchings shared a touching memory of his mother comforting him during a tough time. "Mother's kindness and strength have always been our guiding light," he said. "Her love is the foundation of our family."

Theodore, always the entertainer, had everyone in stitches with his tales of mischievous adventures at the Hermitage. "We may have gotten into trouble more than once," he admitted with a laugh. "But it was all part of growing up with such incredible parents."

Lyncoya, speaking last, expressed his gratitude once more. "Being part of this family has given me more than I could ever have imagined. Thank you, Father and Mother, for your unwavering love."

As the night drew to a close, Andrew and Rachel stood together, watching their guests enjoy the celebration. They felt a deep sense of gratitude and contentment, knowing that their love had brought so many wonderful people into their lives.

Rachel leaned into Andrew; her voice soft. "This has been a perfect day."

Andrew nodded; his eyes filled with love. "It has, my dear. And it's just the beginning of many more to come."

Hand in hand, they walked back to the house, ready to face whatever the future held, surrounded by the love and support of their family and friends.

As the celebration wound down and guests began to depart, Andrew and Rachel Jackson bid their farewells, expressing their gratitude to everyone who had shared in their special day. The moon hung high in the sky as the last of the well-wishers left, and the couple made their way back to the house.

The house was quiet, with only the soft rustle of leaves outside breaking the silence. Andrew and Rachel climbed the stairs to their bedroom, feeling the weight of the day's events settle over them. They were tired but content, their hearts full of the love and support they had received.

Once in their room, Andrew helped Rachel remove the last of her jewelry and unpin her hair. She smiled at him in the mirror, her eyes reflecting the happiness she felt.

"Today was wonderful," Rachel said softly. "Thank you for everything, Andrew."

Andrew turned to her to face him, taking her hands in his. "It was a perfect day because it was spent with you, Rachel."

They changed into their nightclothes and slipped into bed, the familiar comfort of their shared space wrapping around them. Andrew pulled Rachel close, his arm around her shoulders as she rested her head on his chest.

For a moment, they lay in comfortable silence, listening to the sounds of the night. Then, Andrew spoke, his voice filled with deep emotion.

"Rachel, I need you to know something. No matter what happens, no matter what challenges we face, my love for you will always endure. You are the heart of my life, and I am grateful for every moment we have together."

Rachel lifted her head to look into his eyes. "And I love you, Andrew. You are my strength and my refuge. Together, we can face anything."

He kissed her gently, their bond reaffirmed by the day's events. "I promise you, Rachel, I will always be by your side. Our love is stronger than anything the world can throw at us."

Rachel smiled, her eyes glistening with unshed tears. "With you, I believe that."

They settled back down, holding each other close as they drifted into sleep, the peace of their love surrounding them. The future was uncertain, but their commitment to each other was unwavering, and they knew they could face whatever came their way as long as they were together.

As the house grew quiet and the candlelight dimmed, the Hermitage stood as a testament to their enduring love, a beacon of hope and strength in the face of life's many trials. And in that moment, Andrew and Rachel Jackson found solace in the certainty of their love, ready to face the future hand in hand.

Chapter 6

He's More Jefferson

March 17, 1828

In the elegant parlor of the Senate leader's Washington City home, the atmosphere was alive with the animated chatter of congressmen and their wives. The room, adorned with polished mahogany furniture and glistening crystal chandeliers, provided a refined setting for their conversation.

As they sipped on glasses of fine Madeira wine, Congressman Robert Stevens, known for his eloquence, steered the conversation toward the upcoming presidential election. "Ladies and gentlemen, it's an exciting time in our nation's history. The election is approaching swiftly, and our choice will undoubtedly shape our great republic's course."

Margaret Reynolds, the wife of a Congressman and a fervent supporter of Andrew Jackson, chimed in. "Indeed, the people are looking for a leader who embodies their spirit and understands their hopes and dreams. General Jackson is a man of the people, and he'll bring the voice of the common man to the executive mansion."

Congressman Samuel Hawthorne, known for opposing Jackson, offered a dissenting view. "While I respect General Jackson's military achievements, I have reservations about his qualifications for the presidency. We must not overlook the experience and statesmanship that President Adams brings to the table."

The discussion continued, reflecting the broader political landscape of the time. The 1828 election had become a fierce battle, pitting the Jacksonian Democrats against the National Republicans. The issue of whether a military hero like Jackson was better suited for the presidency or whether Adams' diplomatic skills were more crucial took center stage.

Congressman Edward Sinclair, an independent thinker, interjected thoughtfully. "I believe it's important for us to remember that the heart of our democracy lies in the voices of the people. This election is a testament to the vitality of our system. Let the voters decide the path they wish our country to take."

As the conversation ebbed and flowed, the congressmen and their wives expressed their concerns, hopes, and doubts about the upcoming election. It was a reflection of the spirited and sometimes heated discussions taking place in the political arenas of Washington.

During the lively discussion about the upcoming election in the Senate leader's home, a National Republican senator, Richard Stratton, approached the assembled group. Known for his eloquence and political acumen, he had a knack for inserting himself into conversations of importance.

With a warm smile, Senator Stratton joined the circle. "Good evening, ladies and gentlemen. It seems we have a spirited discussion here about the upcoming election."

Congressman Stevens greeted him with a nod. "Indeed, Senator. We're debating the merits of our respective candidates."

Stratton couldn't resist engaging in the discourse. "Well, as we consider the direction of our nation, let's not forget the guidance of our founding fathers. Thomas Jefferson, for instance, would have a clear perspective on this matter. He believed in the strength of the federal government, the importance of diplomacy, and the value of education. President Adams embodies these principles."

Mrs. Reynolds, who had expressed her support for Jackson earlier, responded thoughtfully. "Senator, General Jackson's military leadership and his commitment to the common man are qualities that many believe will serve the country well. It's a different vision for America, one that resonates with the people."

Stratton, undeterred, continued to make his case. "Jefferson also emphasized the value of political unity. President Adams has worked tirelessly to bridge political divides and create a government that reflects the will of the people. He is committed to a vision of an America that is united, strong, and prosperous."

The conversation continued, with Stratton and the others offering their perspectives on the merits of the two candidates. It was a reflection of the broader debates taking place in the political landscape of the time, where supporters of Jackson and Adams passionately argued their cases, drawing on the ideals of the Founding Fathers to support their positions.

As the lively debate over the upcoming election continued in the leader's home, the group had attracted the attention of a familiar face—Senator Martin Van Buren. Van Buren had a shrewd political mind. His ardent support for Andrew Jackson was legendary.

With a determined stride, Van Buren approached the group and joined the conversation. "Evening," he greeted them, acknowledging Senator Stratton and the congressmen.

Congressman Stevens, aware of Van Buren's passionate support for Jackson, offered a nod of recognition. "Senator Van Buren, we were just discussing the presidential election and the principles of our founding fathers. Senator Stratton here was making the argument that Thomas Jefferson would support President Adams."

Van Buren couldn't conceal the passion in his voice as he responded. "Well, you see, Senator Stratton, I can't help but respectfully disagree. President Jefferson believed in the power of the people, in their right to choose their leaders, and in a government that adheres to the principles of democracy. General Jackson embodies those ideals."

Mrs. Reynolds, who had earlier supported Jackson, leaned in. "Senator, would you care to elaborate? How do you see General Jackson reflecting Jefferson's principles?"

Van Buren began to articulate his perspective with fervor. "Jefferson believed in the idea of the common man, the yeoman farmer, as the backbone of our democracy. General Jackson, with his humble beginnings and his commitment to the ordinary citizens, embodies that very spirit. He's a man who has experienced hardship and has dedicated his life to public service, just as Jefferson envisioned."

Senator Stratton, ever the diplomat, offered a measured response. "It's clear that Jefferson's vision was multifaceted, and different aspects of his philosophy may align with various candidates. Our discussion tonight is a testament to the complexities of America."

The conversation continued, with Van Buren passionately making the case that Jefferson's legacy could be seen in Jackson's commitment to the common man and his vision for a government that served the people. The congressmen and their wives listened intently, absorbing the arguments presented by both sides.

In the parlor, the debate between Senators Stratton and Van Buren over who Thomas Jefferson would support in the upcoming presidential election raged. The atmosphere in the grand room became charged with political fervor as both senators presented their arguments.

Stratton leaned into his argument with conviction. "Senator Van Buren, it's clear that Jefferson valued the role of a strong central government. He believed in the importance of diplomatic efforts and the protection of individual liberties. These are values that President Adams upholds, and he has worked tirelessly to unite the country under these principles."

Van Buren, equally fervent in his support of Andrew Jackson, retorted, "Senator Stratton, you mustn't forget that Jefferson was a staunch advocate for the common man, for the agrarian ideals that celebrated the average American. General Jackson, with his background and his commitment to the people, carries on that legacy. He is the embodiment of Jefferson's vision for a government that reflects the will of the people."

The two senators traded arguments with an intensity that reflected the broader political divisions of the time. Stratton highlighted Adams' diplomatic achievements, his efforts to strengthen the federal government, and his commitment to civil liberties. He believed that Adams' experience and knowledge made him the rightful heir to Jefferson's legacy.

Van Buren, on the other hand, emphasized Jackson's humble origins and his dedication to the rights of the common man. He argued that Jackson's military heroism and commitment to the people aligned more closely with Jefferson's vision of a government that remained connected to its citizens.

As the debate continued, it was evident that both senators were deeply committed to their candidates and their respective interpretations of Jefferson's legacy. The room hummed with the exchange of ideas and the clash of political philosophies.

Mrs. Reynolds had been listening attentively, finally interjected. "Gentlemen, it's clear that both candidates have their merits, and the election will be decided by the voice of the people. It's a testament to the strength of America that we can engage in such passionate debates."

Everyone nodded in agreement, recognizing that the clash of ideas was a fundamental aspect of American politics.

Amidst the fervent exchange between the two senators, the Senate leader, a man of distinction and diplomatic finesse, approached the arguing men. His ability to bridge political divides and his measured approach to contentious matters was what made him an effective leader.

"Ladies and gentlemen, if I may," he began, commanding the attention of those present, "I understand the passion that both Senators Stratton and Van Buren bring to this discussion. It's a testament to the vitality of our guests that we can engage in such robust debates. However, let us remember that Thomas Jefferson was a complex figure with multifaceted views."

Both senators turned their attention to the Senate leader, a symbol of wisdom and experience in the political landscape. Stratton and Van Buren listened intently as he continued, "Jefferson's legacy encompasses a broad range of principles. He was a champion of individual liberty, diplomacy, and the power of the people. It's entirely possible that he could have appreciated aspects of both candidates, President Adams and General Jackson."

The Senate leader's words carried the weight of authority, and his diplomatic approach resonated with those present. "In times such as these, when our nation faces crucial choices, it is a reminder that our founding fathers' ideals can be seen through different lenses. We must respect the diversity of opinion that shapes our democracy and honor the will of the American people."

The senators, with their passionate arguments momentarily set aside, nodded in agreement. The congressmen and their wives in the parlor recognized the wisdom in the Senate leader's words. It was a moment that underscored the nuanced nature of American politics and the complexity of the issues at hand.

As the debate ebbed, the Senate leader's guidance provided a moment of reflection. The ongoing political discourse was a testament to the strength of the nation's democratic system, where a variety of voices and opinions converged, all under the watchful gaze of history and the enduring spirit of the nation's founders.

Chapter 7

Trade War

May 25, 1828

Ladies and gentlemen, fellow citizens,

"I stand before you today on the steps of the United States Capitol, a symbol of our great nation's democratic principles and the sanctity of our Constitution. I come before you to address a matter of utmost importance, one that strikes at the heart of our economic well-being and the rights of our citizens."

"It is with a heavy heart and a sense of duty that I must denounce the tariffs recently passed by the House of Representatives. These tariffs are nothing short of an abomination. They are an affront to the principles of free trade and economic liberty that our nation was founded upon."

"The idea of tariffs is not inherently wrong; they can serve as a means to protect our fledgling industries and promote self-sufficiency. However, the rates imposed by this legislation go beyond protection; they are excessive, burdensome, and, yes, an abomination to our nation's economic health."

"These tariffs, my fellow citizens, threaten to divide our great nation. They create economic imbalances, driving a wedge between the different regions of our country. The burdens fall disproportionately on the Southern states, affecting our agricultural and trade-based economy, while favoring the industrial interests of the North."

"We must not forget the principles of our Republic. Our Constitution was designed to protect all citizens' rights, not favor one section of the nation at the expense of another. With their protectionist agenda, these tariffs distort the very essence of our democracy."

"Our founding fathers envisioned a nation that upheld the principles of liberty and equality. They believed in a government that served the interests of all, not just a select few. These tariffs run counter to those principles, benefiting the few at the expense of the many."

"I implore our fellow representatives to reconsider this ill-conceived legislation. Let us remember that we are a united nation, bound together by the ideals of democracy and freedom. We must strive for economic policies that promote the well-being of all citizens and avoid any measure that sows discord and division."

"In closing, I ask for your support in standing against these tariffs of abomination. Let us champion the cause of economic justice, preserving the unity and integrity of our great nation. May we continue to uphold the principles that have made the United States of America a shining example of democracy and opportunity for the world."

A thunderous applause from the assembled crowd erupted as Calhoun finished his speech. As the crowd started to disperse and he was shaking hands with the various supporters gathered, a messenger came up to him and handed him a note telling him it was from

the President. *Come to the Executive Mansion immediately.*
– John Adams

In a private and dimly lit dining room in Washington, Vice President John C. Calhoun, along with his close political ally Martin Van Buren and a gathering of like-minded Democratic senators, gathered for a dinner that held a deeper purpose. The central topic of conversation was clear—the defeat of the tariffs that had recently passed the House of Representatives.

As they sipped on glasses of wine and dined on sumptuous fare, the conversation shifted its focus to strategy. Calhoun, his resolve unwavering, set the tone. "My fellow senators, we find ourselves facing a grave threat to the unity of our nation with these tariffs. We must act decisively and strategically."

Van Buren, his political acumen in full display, interjected. "We need to build a broad coalition of support against these tariffs. It's not just a Southern issue; it affects the entire nation. We should reach out to our Northern counterparts who understand the dangers of economic imbalance."

Senator Elijah Thornton, his eloquently strong stance on free trade clear, added, "We must leverage the power of our words, speaking to the hearts and minds of our fellow senators. We can't allow this legislation to become law, as it would spell disaster for our nation's economic future."

The discussion continued deep into the evening, as they brainstormed ways to build bipartisan opposition to the tariffs. They considered the importance of appealing to the principles of liberty and equality that lay at the heart of the nation's founding, and how to frame the debate in a way that would resonate with senators from all regions.

Calhoun, drawing on his experience as Vice President and his passion for the cause, concluded the evening by saying, "We are stewards of this great nation, and we must protect its integrity and prosperity. Let us continue to gather support, unite our voices, and lead the charge against these tariffs of abomination. We shall prevail in the name of justice and the preservation of our democratic ideals."

The dinner ended with a sense of determination and unity among the Democratic senators. They knew that the battle against the tariffs would be challenging, however with their collective effort and strategic approach, they hoped to defend the principles that had made the United States a beacon of freedom and opportunity for its citizens.

***

In the hallowed halls of the Senate, where the fate of the tariffs hung in the balance, Senator Martin Van Buren was quietly orchestrating a strategic move. He understood the complexities of the political landscape, and he was well aware that, while the tariffs were burdensome to the South, they could also be used as leverage to gain support from Northern senators.

Van Buren, a political tactician with a pragmatic approach, had been working behind the scenes with a small but influential group of senators from the North. They planned to propose amendments to the tariff legislation, introducing import tariffs on raw goods vital to Northern factories. The goal was to make the tariffs unpalatable to Northern senators, pushing them to vote against the entire package.

Senator William Anderson, a representative of Northern industrial interests, spoke to Van Buren about the proposed amendments. "Senator Van Buren, this is a risky move. We need to convince our colleagues from the North that these tariffs will harm our industries. Are you confident this strategy will work?"

Van Buren, a shrewd negotiator, replied, "Senator Anderson, we must create a united front against these tariffs. By adding import tariffs on the raw materials our factories depend on, we'll demonstrate that this legislation is detrimental to both the North and the South. It's a calculated risk, but it's one we must take."

The senators from the North were apprehensive but agreed to move forward with the plan. Together, they drafted amendments that introduced import tariffs on iron, wool, and other raw materials used by Northern factories. Their message was clear: these tariffs would hinder the growth of Northern industry and cost jobs.

When the amendments were introduced in committee, Van Buren and his allies argued passionately for their inclusion. They cited the potential harm to northern businesses, emphasizing the importance of preserving economic growth and safeguarding the welfare of their constituents.

Northern senators, initially supportive of the tariffs, began to express doubts. The amendments struck a chord, and they recognized the economic consequences of the legislation. Van Buren and his allies continued to work behind the scenes, lobbying their northern colleagues to join the opposition against the tariffs.

As the debate over the tariffs intensified, the amendments introduced by Van Buren and his allies became a focal point. The northern senators who had once supported the tariffs now found themselves questioning the wisdom of the legislation.

The strategic move by Senator Martin Van Buren had proven effective in building a broad coalition of opposition, uniting senators from both the North and the South in their determination to protect the principles of economic prosperity upon which the nation was founded. It was a testament to the power of political strategy and the commitment of senators to safeguard the interests of their constituents and the nation as a whole, however, it wasn't enough to keep the legislation from passing out of committee and to the floor of the full Senate.

The tariffs took center stage as the senators engaged in a passionate floor debate the following week. The atmosphere was charged with tension and anticipation, with senators from various regions of the country eager to make their case.

Senator Martin Van Buren, a staunch critic of the tariffs, rose to address his colleagues. "My fellow senators, these tariffs, as they stand, threaten the unity of our great nation. They are excessive, burdensome, and disruptive to our economic well-being. We cannot allow this legislation to pass."

Senator William Anderson countered, "Senator Van Buren, we understand your concerns, but these tariffs are necessary to protect our industries and provide jobs for our constituents. We must support our factories and promote domestic production."

As the debate raged on, senators from the South and the North presented their arguments, reflecting the deep divide on the issue. The southern senators argued that the tariffs disproportionately burdened their region, while their northern counterparts defended the need for protectionism.

Senator Thornton emphasized the impact of the tariffs on the common man. "We cannot overlook that these tariffs will harm our citizens, especially those with limited means. We must ensure that the principles of democracy and economic justice prevail."

Senator Samuel Hamilton, an advocate for the tariffs, retorted, "Senator, we must protect our industries and promote self-sufficiency. These tariffs will strengthen our nation and prevent foreign domination of our markets."

The floor debate continued for hours, with senators passionately expressing their views and attempting to persuade their colleagues. The stakes were high, as the decision on the tariffs had far-reaching implications for the nation's economic future.

As the debate drew to a close, the vote on the tariffs approached. It was evident that the division in the Senate mirrored the broader divisions in the nation, with senators from different regions and interests fiercely advocating for their constituents and their vision of America's economic future.

The floor debate had been a vivid illustration of the complexities of American politics, where competing interests, principles, and visions converged in the pursuit of a brighter future for the young nation.

The vote on the contentious legislation had finally reached its moment of decision. Senators from various regions of the country had gathered, their seats filled with anticipation and trepidation.

Vice President John Calhoun presided over the session. He had labored tirelessly behind the scenes, working to defeat the legislation that he believed would harm the southern economy.

The debate that had raged in the Senate chamber in the days leading up to the vote had revealed the stark divisions within the nation. Southern senators, led by Calhoun, had argued vehemently against the tariffs, asserting that they were burdensome and detrimental to the interests of their constituents. Northern senators, representing the industrial interests of their region, had countered that the tariffs were necessary to protect American industries and provide jobs.

As the Senate began to vote, each senator's name was called, and they rose to cast their ballots. The tension in the chamber was palpable as the fate of the tariffs hung in the balance.

Senator Martin Van Buren, a key ally of Calhoun and a prominent figure within the Democratic Party, exchanged knowing glances with his colleagues. They had worked tirelessly to build a coalition of opposition, reaching out to senators from both the

North and the South who recognized the potential harm of the tariffs.

One by one, the senators voted, their voices echoing through the chamber. The count began, and the outcome remained uncertain until the very end. When the final votes were tallied, the result was a narrow victory for the tariffs.

A hushed silence filled the chamber as the verdict was announced. The opponents of the tariffs, including Calhoun and Van Buren, held their breath, their efforts and determination rewarded with defeat.

As the senators filed out of the chamber, there was a sense of both relief and accomplishment among those who had opposed the tariffs. The battle over economic policies and principles had been hard-fought, but it was a testament to the strength of their cause.

After the disheartening passage of the tariffs, the Vice President, along with his political ally Martin Van Buren and a group of Democratic senators, gathered for a private dinner in a dimly lit Washington restaurant. The room, despite its elegant decor, was filled with an air of frustration and disappointment.

Calhoun, whose efforts to defeat the tariffs had fallen short, sat at the head of the table, his face etched with a rare display of anger and frustration. He addressed his colleagues, his voice tinged with bitterness. "My friends, I cannot express the depth of my frustration and anger at the passage of these tariffs. They threaten the unity of our nation and harm the interests of our constituents."

Senator Martin Van Buren, who had worked tirelessly alongside Calhoun, nodded in agreement. "It's disheartening, to say the least. We must remember, however, that the battle is not over. Our commitment to defending our principles and economic justice remains steadfast."

Other Democratic senators shared their sentiments of disappointment and frustration, understanding the magnitude of the challenge they faced. The tariffs were now law, and the battle to protect their constituents' interests continued.

Calhoun took a deep breath, his frustration palpable. "We must continue to build a coalition of opposition. Our mission is to ensure that the damaging impact of these tariffs is recognized, and that the American people's interests are safeguarded."

The group of Democratic senators nodded in agreement; their determination unwavering. The passage of the tariffs may have been a setback, but it had not deterred their commitment to preserving the principles upon which the nation was founded.

As the evening wore on, the dinner conversation shifted from frustration to a renewed sense of purpose. The senators understood that their work was far from over, and that they had a duty to their constituents and for the nation as a whole.

The tariffs may have been a bitter pill to swallow, but they also served as a rallying point for those who believed in the principles of the United States. The dinner concluded with a shared determination to continue the fight, recognizing that the battle for the nation's future was far from finished.

Chapter 8

A Devastating Loss

July 11, 1828

Andrew Jackson and Martin Van Buren met for breakfast at a local tavern in Washington City in the early morning light of this warm day. The tavern, with its bustling atmosphere, was a place where local and visiting politicians often gathered to discuss matters of state and strategy.

Jackson and Van Buren were well acquainted, and their friendship extended beyond the confines of politics. Both men had grown close during their time serving in the Senate, sharing a mutual commitment to democratic principles. This morning, however, their conversation was focused on the upcoming presidential election and the strategy needed to secure Jackson's victory.

As they sat at a corner table, sipping on coffee and enjoying their morning meal, the hostess of the tavern, a woman of warm hospitality, approached their table. She held a sealed letter and extended it to Jackson with a smile.

"Good morning, General Jackson," she greeted him. "This just arrived for you. It appears to be from your home."

Jackson couldn't hide a trace of warmth as he accepted the letter. "Thank you kindly, ma'am," he said, as he broke the seal and unfolded the parchment.

Van Buren watched with genuine curiosity as Jackson's expression changed while reading the letter. The General's countenance shifted from his usual stern composure to one of surprise and, eventually, a soft frown.

Van Buren leaned in, unable to contain his curiosity. "General, is there news from home?"

Jackson nodded, a glint of pride in his eyes. "Indeed, there is. It's a letter from Rachel, and she tells me that our son, Lyncoya has fallen ill at the Hermitage."

Van Buren shared in Jackson's concern, offering his condolences and well wishes. "General, I'm sorry to hear that, and I pray for a speedy and complete recovery of his health."

Jackson's frown remained, and he folded the letter with care, tucking it safely in his coat pocket. "Thank you. It's a reminder that life is precious and what we're fighting for in this upcoming election—the future of our families, our nation, and the principles we hold dear."

As Andrew Jackson and his campaign manager left the bustling tavern after their breakfast with Van Buren, their conversation continued. The morning sunbathed the streets of Washington City in a warm glow.

Francis Williamson chimed in first "General, that breakfast with Martin went well. Van Buren is an astute political strategist, and his support will be invaluable in the upcoming election. We must build a strong coalition to secure your victory."

Andrew Jackson nodded, acknowledging the importance of the alliance they were forging with Van Buren and other key political figures. "You're right, and I'm grateful for his support. We're in for a challenging battle against Adams, and we need all the support we can get."

As they walked, Jackson began to open the letter from Rachel. The parchment felt delicate in his hands, and he was eager to read her words. However, as he began to read, his steps slowed, and he stopped in his tracks. Williamson noticed his sudden change in demeanor.

"General, is something the matter? What does the letter say?"

Jackson's eyes remained fixed on the letter, and he slowly looked up at his campaign manager, his expression a mix of surprise and concern. "It says...

that Lyncoya is not well. He's fallen seriously ill, and they're doing everything they can to save him."

The campaign manager expressed his sympathies and support. "I'm so sorry to hear that, General. We should make arrangements to return to the Hermitage as soon as possible."

Jackson nodded, his thoughts already racing ahead. "Yes, we must leave for Tennessee immediately. Family comes first, and I won't be at peace until I'm by Rachel's side. The campaign will have to wait."

With a heavy heart, Jackson folded the letter and carefully tucked it away, a reminder of the unforeseen challenges that life could bring. The upcoming election, the politics, and the campaign would need to be put on hold for the time being, as the urgent call of family and a child in need took precedence.

***

My Dearest Andrew,

I hope this letter finds you in Washington City, amidst your political duties and responsibilities. I am writing to you with a heavy heart, burdened by news that I wish I could deliver to you in person.

Our dear Lyncoya, our cherished native son, has fallen ill with consumption, and his condition is dire. His little body has been ravaged by this terrible disease, and he is fighting with the strength of a warrior, but the odds are against him.

The doctors have been attending to him with the utmost care, and I have not left his side, praying for a miracle to save him. Our Lyncoya, the son we welcomed into our hearts, is in great pain, and it breaks my heart to see him suffer.

I know how much you love him, and it pains me that you cannot be here with us during this trying time. I long for your comforting presence and your strong embrace to help us through this difficult ordeal.

The days are long, Andrew, and the nights are even longer. I cannot help but think of you and wish that you were here to share this burden with me. Your love and support have always been my strength, and I know that you love Lyncoya as if he were your flesh and blood.

I will keep you updated on his condition, but I wanted you to know the gravity of the situation. Please, my dear husband, if there is any way you can return home, I implore you to do so. Your presence would mean the world to both Lyncoya and me.

I understand the importance of your political endeavors and the upcoming election, but our son needs you, and I need you. Family comes before all else, and I believe you would agree that being by our son's side in his time of need is the most important duty of all.

I long to see you, to share our hopes and our fears, and to face this trial as a family. Please consider returning to us as soon as you can. We need you more than ever, my love.

With all my heart and longing for your presence,

Rachel

***

Jackson, having received Rachel's distressing letter about Lyncoya, felt the weight of concern settle heavily upon him. The political matters in Washington City, once urgent and pressing, now paled in comparison to the well-being of his son. The decision was clear—he needed to be with his family at the Hermitage.

With a heavy heart, Jackson called for his campaign manager and other key advisors to his quarters. They entered, finding him sitting at a sturdy wooden desk, his brow furrowed with worry.

"General Jackson, what brings you to such solemn reflection? Is there news from the home?"

Jackson nodded, a somber expression on his face. "Rachel has written to me. Lyncoya is terribly ill with consumption. The situation is dire, and I must return to home immediately."

His campaign manager, recognizing the gravity of the situation, offered his understanding. "General, family comes first. We will make the necessary arrangements for your return. The campaign will continue in your absence."

Jackson, grateful for the support, took a deep breath. "I appreciate your understanding. My family needs me, and I cannot turn a blind eye to their suffering. Please, help me organize my departure as swiftly as possible."

The campaign manager nodded, already thinking ahead. "We'll secure transportation and inform those involved in your political affairs. Your presence at the Hermitage is undoubtedly where you need to be."

In the moments that followed, Jackson moved with a sense of urgency. He canceled scheduled meetings, informed key political allies of his departure, and penned a letter to Martin Van Buren, expressing his regret for leaving during this crucial time in the campaign. The affairs of the nation would have to wait; his duty as a husband and father took precedence.

As he prepared to leave Washington City, a mix of emotions filled Jackson. The weight of political responsibility hung over him, but the pull of family was stronger. He found solace in knowing that those he left behind understood the gravity of the situation.

In the bustling streets around him, Angus Smith, Jackson's trusted advisor and close friend, received an urgent message about Lyncoya's grave illness. The weight of the news hung heavy on his shoulders as he understood the gravity of the situation. He knew that his duty was not only to the General but also to the Jackson family.

Angus immediately began making arrangements for his journey back to Tennessee. As he entered the room where the General was preparing for his departure, he found the atmosphere heavy with concern.

Angus started "General, I've received word about Lyncoya. I'm sorry to hear about his condition. I'm ready to make the necessary arrangements for our journey back to the Hermitage."

Jackson, in the midst of packing, looked up with a mixture of gratitude and distress. "Angus, your support means a great deal to me. We need to return to home as quickly as possible. Lyncoya needs us, and Rachel mustn't face this ordeal alone."

Angus nodded, understanding the depth of the situation. "I've secured a carriage for our journey back. It's waiting for us outside. We should make haste, General, every moment counts."

As they stepped into the waiting carriage, the gravity of the situation weighed on both men. The streets of Washington City, once a place of political fervor, now seemed distant and inconsequential compared to the personal trial unfolding back home.

The journey back to Tennessee was marked by an uneasy silence. Andrew Jackson, normally a man of firm resolve, was visibly shaken by the uncertainty surrounding Lyncoya's health. Angus, sensing the weight on his friend's shoulders, offered words of comfort and reassurance.

"General, we'll get you home soon. Your family needs you, and Lyncoya needs our strength. We'll be by their side, come what may."

Jackson, looking out at the passing landscape, nodded. "You're right, Angus. Family is everything. I just hope we get there in time."

As they neared the Hermitage, the air became heavy with anticipation and anxiety. The familiar sight of the plantation brought a mix of emotions—relief at being home and anguish over what awaited them. The carriage rolled to a stop, and both men hurriedly disembarked, ready to face the challenges that awaited them within the walls.

As Jackson's carriage rolled through the gates of the home, a heaviness settled over the plantation. The air, once filled with the sounds of nature and the bustling energy of a thriving homestead, now carried a somber stillness. The news of Lyncoya's passing had cast a pall over the familiar landscape.

As the carriage came to a stop, Jackson stepped out, his usual air of strength and determination replaced by a profound grief. Angus, who had been a steadfast companion throughout the journey, followed close behind. The two men exchanged a solemn glance, acknowledging the weight of the moment.

"Angus, I wish I could have been here sooner. I wanted to be by Lyncoya's side."

Angus, equally affected by the tragedy, placed a comforting hand on Jackson's shoulder. "General, you did everything you could. Lyncoya knew he was loved. Now, we must be there for Rachel and the family."

As they entered the homestead, the atmosphere was thick with sorrow. Family members moved about quietly, their expressions a mix of grief and a shared understanding of the pain that had befallen them.

Rachel, who had been a constant presence at Lyncoya's bedside, now sat in a dimly lit room, her eyes red from tears.

Andrew approached his wife, his heart heavy with the weight of the news he already knew. He kneeled beside her, taking her hand in his. No words were exchanged—only a shared, silent acknowledgment of the profound loss they now faced together.

Rachel, her voice trembling with grief, spoke softly. "Andrew, he... he passed peacefully. I held his hand, and he knew we were with him."

Jackson, overcome with sorrow, held Rachel close. The room seemed to close in around them as the reality of Lyncoya's absence settled in. He spoke in a hushed voice, his words carrying the weight of regret.

"I should have been here. I should have been here for him, for you."

Rachel, her eyes filled with both sadness and understanding, whispered, "You did what you could, my love. Lyncoya knew you loved him. He knew he was a part of this family."

In the days that followed, the Hermitage became a place of mourning. The once vibrant plantation felt subdued, its spirit dampened by the loss of a young life. Jackson found himself grappling with the pain of not being present during Lyncoya's last moments.

The family gathered to bid farewell to their adopted son. The ceremony was a solemn affair, marked by tears and shared memories of Lyncoya's short but impactful presence in their lives.

As they stood by the grave, Andrew Jackson, his eyes reflecting the grief within, whispered a final goodbye to Lyncoya. The weight of loss lingered, but so did the resolve to honor the memory of the young boy who had become an integral part of the Jackson family.

The Hermitage, once a place of joy and laughter, now carried the echoes of sorrow. And as Jackson faced the challenge of reconciling his absence during Lyncoya's last moments, the bond of family, tested by tragedy, became a source of strength as they navigated the difficult days ahead.

Chapter 9

A Close Call

July 26, 1828

The Nashville Inn buzzed with the clatter of dishes and the murmur of morning conversations as Andrew Jackson, his campaign manager, Congressman Davey Crockett, and the Speaker of the Tennessee House of Representatives, Robert Nelson, finished their breakfast. The room was filled with the aroma of fresh coffee and warm biscuits, setting a comfortable backdrop for their morning discussion.

Jackson set his coffee cup down with a decisive clink. "Gentlemen, we've got a long day ahead. Let's make sure we're prepared for these meetings. Francis, how's our strategy looking for the rally this afternoon?"

Francis nodded, adjusting his spectacles. "We're on track, General. The turnout is expected to be substantial, and we've got our key talking points lined up. I suggest we focus on the tariff issues and the corruption in the Adams administration."

"Good," Jackson replied, his expression determined. "Nelson, what's the latest from the legislature?"

Nelson leaned forward; his tone conspiratorial. "Support is solid. We've got a majority backing your campaign, and the recent resolution against the Tariffs of Abomination has galvanized a lot of folks. They see you as the champion of the people's rights."

Crockett, who had been quietly finishing his plate, chimed in with his characteristic drawl. "I'll tell ya, General, folks out there are fired up. They ain't gonna take kindly to Adams' tricks. They're lookin' to you to set things straight."

Jackson's face softened with a rare smile. "Thank you, Davey. Your support means a great deal to me."

As they rose from the table and made their way to the door, Crockett's keen hunter's eyes caught sight of a shadowy figure moving suspiciously in the distance, slipping between the buildings across the street. He halted abruptly, causing the others to stop and follow his gaze.

"Hold on, fellas," Crockett said, his voice low and cautious. "Looks like we've got company. See that feller over there?"

Jackson squinted in the direction Crockett indicated. "You think he's trouble, Davey?"

Crockett nodded slowly. "Could be. Ain't no harm in being cautious."

Nelson, always practical, suggested, "Perhaps we should take a different route. No need to invite trouble, especially with so much at stake."

Francis glanced nervously at Jackson. "What do you think, General?"

Jackson's eyes narrowed, a steely resolve hardening his features. "We won't be deterred by shadows. Let's proceed as planned but stay alert. Francis, keep an eye on our surroundings. Davey, stay close."

They stepped out into the crisp morning air, the sun casting long shadows down the bustling street. The men moved with purpose; their senses heightened by Crockett's observation. As they walked, they discussed the day's agenda, their conversation punctuated by the occasional glance over their shoulders.

"First stop is the courthouse," Francis reminded them. "We've got a meeting with the local leaders to discuss voter mobilization."

Crockett, still scanning the area, added, "After that, we head to the rally. I'll keep an eye out for any more suspicious activity."

Jackson nodded. "Let's not let anything distract us from our goal. We need to show the people we're committed to their cause, no matter what the obstacles are."

As they approached the courthouse, the shadowy figure reappeared, watching from a distance. Jackson's group ignored the figure, their focus unwavering. The morning passed in a series of productive meetings, each one reinforcing their strategy and bolstering their resolve.

By the time they reached the rally in the afternoon, the shadowy figure had disappeared, leaving the men to concentrate on their mission. As Jackson took the stage to address the crowd, his voice rang out with conviction, inspiring those gathered to support his bid for the presidency.

The group exited the rally and started down the bustling street, each man deep in thought about the day's events. The air was crisp, and the sunlight filtered through the trees lining the road, casting dappled shadows on the cobblestones.

Crockett, ever vigilant, scanned the crowd. "Just keep your eyes peeled, fellas. We might have some unwanted attention."

As they walked, Jackson, with his tall, commanding presence, drew the eyes of passersby. Many tipped their hats or offered respectful nods. Jackson acknowledged each gesture with a nod, his mind focused on the tasks at hand.

"General," Nelson said, breaking the silence, "it's vital we address the concerns about the tariffs. People are feeling the pinch."

"Agreed," Jackson replied. "We need to make it clear that we're fighting for the common man. Adams' policies are strangling the livelihood of our farmers and tradesmen."

Francis, adjusting his glasses, added, "And we must highlight the corruption. The people need to know about the underhanded deals that have kept Adams in power."

Just then, Crockett's sharp eyes caught movement. The shadowy figure he had spotted earlier was now stealthily moving closer, slipping between the throngs of people. He subtly nudged Jackson's arm and nodded toward the figure.

"He's getting bolder, General," Crockett said quietly. "We might have a situation on our hands."

Jackson's eyes narrowed. "Stay close, gentlemen. We'll handle this if it comes to it."

They continued down the street, the figure gradually closing the distance. Jackson's mind raced through possible scenarios. Was it a spy from the Adams camp? A potential assassin? The tension was palpable, but he maintained a calm exterior.

As they neared the courthouse, the figure was just a few yards behind them. Crockett, sensing imminent danger, whispered, "Let's take that alley to the right. We can confront him there."

The group veered into the alleyway, the sounds of the busy street fading behind them. The figure, realizing they had altered their path, quickened his pace.

"Now," Crockett said, spinning around to face the approaching figure, his hand resting on the hilt of his knife. "Who are you, and why are you following us?"

The figure halted, momentarily startled. It was a young man, no more than twenty, with a nervous look on his face. He raised his hands in a gesture of surrender.

"Please, don't hurt me," the young man pleaded. "I'm just a messenger. I have a note for General Jackson."

Jackson stepped forward, his eyes scrutinizing the messenger. "Who sent you?"

The young man fumbled in his coat pocket and pulled out a folded piece of paper, extending it to Jackson with a trembling hand. "I don't know, sir. I was paid to deliver this to you, and to make sure no one saw me."

Jackson took the note, his eyes never leaving the messenger's face. "What's your name, son?"

"James, sir. James Porter."

Jackson nodded, unfolding the paper. As he read, his expression grew stern. He handed the note to Francis. "It's a warning. Someone's planning to disrupt the campaign."

Francis scanned the note quickly. "We need to take this seriously. If they're planning violence, we need to be prepared."

Crockett looked at James. "How much do you know about this plan?"

James shook his head. "Nothing, sir. I swear. I was just paid to deliver the message."

Nelson, stepping closer, said, "We should get him somewhere safe, just in case. And we need to alert the local authorities."

Jackson agreed. "Take James to a secure location. Nelson, go with him and ensure he's not harmed. The rest of us will proceed to the courthouse and then plan our response."

As Nelson led the young messenger away, Jackson, Francis, and Crokett continued toward the courthouse, the weight of the note's warning heavy on their minds.

"This changes our approach," Jackson said. "We need to be vigilant and ensure the safety of our supporters."

Francis nodded. "I'll arrange for extra security. We can't let fear dictate our actions."

Jackson's eyes blazed with determination. "Agreed. We'll show them that we won't be intimidated. The people's voice will be heard."

As Jackson, Williamson, Crockett, and Nelson, who had just rejoined the group, emerged from the courthouse, the tension from the warning note still hung in the air. They were discussing their next steps when suddenly, a shadowy figure appeared, this time rushing directly toward them.

Before anyone could react, the man pulled out a pistol and aimed it straight at Jackson's head. The hammer clicked, but the gun didn't fire. For a moment, time seemed to stand still, and the group was frozen in shock.

"What in tarnation!" Crockett exclaimed, breaking the silence.

The would-be assassin, his face twisted in frustration, pulled out another pistol with trembling hands. He aimed again, but once more, the gun jammed.

Jackson's eyes blazed with fury. "You vile coward!" he roared, raising his walking cane high. With a swift and powerful motion, he brought it down on the man's head.

The assailant staggered, but Jackson did not relent. He continued to beat him with the cane, each strike fueled by righteous anger. Crockett and Williamson quickly sprang into action, wrestling the man to the ground as Jackson stepped back, still brandishing his cane.

"Hold him down!" Crockett shouted, pinning the man's arms behind his back. Williamson, using his considerable strength, held the man's legs.

Nelson, recovering from the initial shock, bellowed, "Police! Police, over here!"

A nearby constable, hearing the commotion, ran toward the group. "What's happening here?" he demanded, eyes wide at the sight of the scuffle.

"This man just tried to kill General Jackson!" Nelson shouted, pointing at the assailant. "He pulled a gun on him twice!"

The constable quickly secured the man in cuffs, his face pale. "General Jackson, are you all right, sir?"

Jackson, breathing heavily, nodded. "I'm fine, officer. Thanks to my friends here. Take this scoundrel away and make sure he's locked up tight."

As the constable led the would-be assassin away, a crowd began to gather, murmuring and pointing. News of the attack spread quickly, and soon more police arrived to manage the scene.

Crockett, wiping his brow, looked at Jackson. "That was a close one, General. Those guns misfiring was a stroke of luck."

Jackson, still gripping his cane, nodded. "Indeed. But we can't rely on luck. We need to be even more vigilant. If this is the extent they're willing to go, we must be prepared for anything."

Williamson, straightening his coat, added, "We'll increase security at all events. And we should investigate who sent this man and why."

Nelson agreed. "This attack is just another sign of the desperation and corruption we're up against. We must remain united and focused."

Jackson, calming down, placed a hand on each of their shoulders. "Thank you, my friends. Your quick actions saved my life today. Let's move forward, with even greater resolve, to fight for our cause."

The group continued on their way, more determined than ever to protect Jackson and secure his place as a leader of the people. The shadow of the attack would linger, but it also galvanized their commitment to justice and the fight against corruption.

Chapter 10

Go West Young Man

August 1, 1828

In the vibrant city of St. Louis, amidst the buzz of commerce and the promise of new horizons, a young family prepared to embark on a journey that would take them to the untamed frontier. The latest month brought the Smith family a sense of adventure and anticipation as they readied themselves to load up their wagons and set out westward.

The sun cast a warm glow over the bustling city streets, where merchants peddled their goods, and the lively chatter of passersby filled the air. In a modest dwelling on the outskirts of town, the Smith family went about their preparations. The patriarch, Samuel Smith, a rugged man with a determination etched into the lines of his face, oversaw the loading of supplies onto the sturdy wooden wagons.

"Sarah, make sure the children have enough blankets and food for the journey. We don't know what lies ahead on the frontier, but we'll be prepared for anything."

Sarah, a resilient woman with a nurturing spirit, bustled about the homestead, ensuring that every necessity was accounted for. Her eyes sparkled with a mix of excitement and the weight of responsibility.

Sarah responded, "I've packed extra provisions, and the children's clothes are neatly stowed away. We'll make the journey safely, Samuel, and build a new life for ourselves out there."

Their two children, Emily and Thomas, played nearby, their youthful enthusiasm evident in every step and giggle. Samuel approached them, kneeling to their level.

"You ready for an adventure, my little pioneers?" Samuel asked his children.

Emily, her eyes wide with curiosity, nodded vigorously. "Yes, Papa! I want to see mountains and rivers and maybe even a real cowboy!"

Thomas, a bit younger but equally excited, chimed in, "And I want to catch a big fish in a real river, Papa!"

Samuel chuckled, ruffling their hair affectionately. "Well, you might just get your wishes, my darlings. Now, let's finish loading up. We've got a long journey ahead."

The wagons, sturdy and well-worn from previous travels, were packed with essentials—bedrolls, cooking utensils, and the few sentimental belongings that the Smith family couldn't bear to part with. A team of oxen waited patiently, harnessed and ready to pull the loaded wagons across the vast expanse of land before them.

The morning sun cast a golden hue over the city as the Smith family gathered for a final breakfast at the boarding house that had been their temporary home. The aroma of freshly brewed coffee and sizzling bacon filled the air as Samuel unfolded the morning newspaper.

Around the worn wooden table, Samuel, his wife Sarah, and their two children sat quietly, contemplating the journey that awaited them. The room, adorned with simple furnishings, held an air of both excitement and trepidation.

"Well, my loves, this is it. Our last breakfast in St. Louis. Soon, we'll be on the trail to the western frontier." Samuel started off the conversation.

Sarah, pouring steaming coffee into worn mugs, smiled at her family. "It's a new beginning, Samuel. A chance for us to build something of our own."

Emily, her eyes wide with wonder, glanced at the window overlooking the bustling city streets. "Papa, are we going to see mountains and rivers like I read in my books?"

Samuel chuckled, ruffling Emily's hair. "That's the plan, sweetheart. The frontier holds all sorts of wonders for us. Now, let's eat up. We've got a long day ahead."

As they enjoyed their breakfast, the clatter of plates and the occasional laughter from other boarders in the house provided a backdrop to their contemplative conversation. Samuel reached for the folded newspaper that had been left on the sideboard and began perusing the headlines.

"Listen to this. The headline says, 'Should America move west?' Seems like folks are pondering the very same question we've been answering for ourselves."

Sarah, wiping her hands on her apron, looked over at Samuel. "What does it say? Is it about people like us, seeking a new life out west?"

Samuel cleared his throat, his eyes scanning the article. "It talks about the vastness of the western territories, and the opportunities for those willing to brave the unknown. Some argue it's our duty as Americans to expand westward, while others caution about the challenges and dangers."

Thomas crumbs on his face from a hearty bite of toast, piped up, "Papa, are we pioneers?"

Samuel grinned, nodding. "Yes, Thomas, we are. We're pioneers heading into the great unknown, just like those who came before us. And we're doing it together as a family."

The family continued to discuss the possibilities and uncertainties ahead as they finished their breakfast. The clinking of utensils against plates and the hum of conversation filled the room, creating a bittersweet symphony of departure.

After the meal, Samuel folded the newspaper and tucked it under his arm. The Smith family gathered their belongings, and with a final glance around the boarding house that had briefly been their home, they stepped out into the sunlit streets of St. Louis.

As they walked towards the waiting wagons, the headline lingered in Samuel's mind—Should America move west? The Smiths, with their hearts full of hope and determination, were already answering that question with each step toward the frontier.

****

The morning sunbathed the Hermitage in a warm glow, and the birdsong outside created a tranquil backdrop to the breakfast table where Andrew Jackson sat, his brows furrowed as he finished reading a newspaper article titled "Should America Move West?" The article, arguing against further Western expansion, had struck a nerve with Old Hickory himself.

The room, adorned with simple yet elegant furnishings, was filled with the comforting aroma of freshly brewed coffee and the clinking of utensils against porcelain. Rachel moved gracefully about the table, ensuring that all was for her husband's morning meal.

"Andrew, dear, your breakfast is ready. I hope you enjoy the eggs. Fresh from our hens this morning."

Jackson, his piercing blue eyes still fixed on the newspaper, grunted in acknowledgment. He had always relished the quiet moments at the breakfast table, but today was different. The article had stirred a fire within him—a fire fueled by the memories of his own frontiersman past.

As Rachel sat down across from him, Andrew set the newspaper aside and took a sip of the steaming coffee. His expression was one of contemplation, mixed with a hint of agitation.

"Rachel, did you read this article? 'Should America Move West?' Can you believe they're suggesting we put a halt to expansion? It's preposterous!"

Rachel, ever the calming influence, spoke with a measured tone. "What has upset you so, Andrew? You've always been a champion of Western expansion."

"It's the audacity of it, Rachel. They argue that the West should be left as it is, untouched. As if the very spirit of America isn't found in the untamed wilderness. These folks, sitting comfortably in their parlors, have no idea what it means to be a frontiersman."

Rachel reached across the table, her hand resting on his. "You are a frontiersman, my love, and you've fought for the expansion of this great nation. Your connection to the West is deep-rooted."

Jackson sighed; his frustration evident. "I've fought in the war, faced the British in the West. I've battled the Creek Indians, securing the safety of our people. The West is in my blood, Rachel, and to suggest we halt its growth is an affront to everything I believe in."

"Perhaps they don't understand the sacrifices made, the struggles faced by those who ventured into the unknown. Your legacy is tied to the West, Andrew, and the people recognize that."

Jackson nodded, his eyes reflecting a mixture of pride and frustration. "You're right, Rachel. The West is the heart of this nation, and I won't stand idly by while they suggest otherwise. I'll make sure our voice is heard."

As they continued their breakfast, the atmosphere in the room shifted. Old Hickory, fueled by a renewed sense of purpose, began to formulate a response to the article that questioned the very essence of his identity—a frontiersman who had dedicated his life to the pursuit of a boundless America.

***

The morning poured through the windows of the Executive Mansion, casting a warm glow over the breakfast table where the President sat. The morning papers lay artfully arranged, and Adams picked up a particularly intriguing one titled "Should America Go West?" The article, advocating for a halt to further Western expansion, caught his attention.

As Adams read through the well-articulated arguments, he found himself nodding in agreement with the author's perspective. The notion of preserving the existing territories and focusing on the development of established regions resonated with his vision for the nation's future.

Louisa Catherine, the first lady, joined him at the table, noticing the thoughtful expression on her husband's face. "John, what has captured your attention in the papers this morning?"

Adams looked up, a hint of contemplation in his eyes. "It's an article discussing whether America should continue expanding westward. The author argues for a more conservative approach, suggesting that perhaps it's time to consolidate rather than constantly push the frontier."

"An interesting perspective. What are your thoughts on the matter, John?"

Adams set the newspaper down and took a sip of his coffee, contemplating his response. "There's merit in the argument. We've pushed the frontier westward for decades, but perhaps it's time to focus on the development and prosperity of the territories we already have."

Louisa nodded, her dark eyes reflecting understanding. "Preserving what we have, investing in the well-being of our existing territories, and fostering stability might indeed be a prudent course of action."

"Exactly. It's a departure from the traditional belief in Manifest Destiny, but it's a perspective that acknowledges the challenges of constant expansion."

As they continued their breakfast, Adams began to form a plan. "I'm considering writing an opinion piece supporting this position. It's time to have a frank discussion with the American people about the future direction of our nation."

Louisa, supportive as ever, smiled. "A well-reasoned opinion from the President might sway public opinion. It's a bold move, John, one that might shape the discourse on our nation's destiny."

Adams, finishing his breakfast, rose from the table with a sense of purpose. "I'll draft a statement today. It's time to challenge conventional wisdom and present a vision for an America that isn't solely defined by its relentless expansion westward."

In the hours that followed, Adams immersed himself in crafting the opinion piece. The document aimed to engage the nation in a thoughtful dialogue about its future, challenging preconceived notions and advocating for a more measured approach to territorial growth.

As the ink dried on the final draft, Adams felt a sense of conviction. It was a departure from the conventional wisdom of the time, but he believed in the power of discourse and the necessity of evolving perspectives to meet the ever-changing needs of the young Republic. The article, signed by the President himself, would soon make its way into newspapers across the country, sparking conversations and perhaps reshaping the nation's trajectory.

Chapter 11

The Written Debates

August 1, 1828

The Executive Mansion was abuzz with the energy of a nation in the midst of change. President Adams, having just finished reading the article questioning further western expansion, felt a stirring within him. The ideas presented resonated with a part of him that had long grappled with the consequences of unrestrained growth.

Adams, a man of introspection and intellectual curiosity, was drawn to the idea of challenging the prevailing sentiment that had driven American expansion for decades. He paced the grand corridors of the mansion, his mind alive with the possibilities of influencing public opinion through the power of the pen.

As he entered his office, Adams summoned his secretary, Charles, with a decisive wave.

"Charles, clear my schedule for the morning. I have something I must attend to."

Charles, accustomed to the President's moments of inspiration, nodded and quickly set about rearranging the day's appointments.

Seated at his desk, Adams gathered his thoughts. The quill pen in his hand seemed to beckon him to put ink to paper, to articulate the vision that had formed in his mind. The President's commitment to thoughtful governance and his belief in the evolving nature of the nation's destiny converged in this moment.

Adams began to write, the words flowing onto the parchment with a purposeful clarity. He crafted an opinion that challenged the notion of relentless western expansion, arguing for a shift in focus toward the consolidation and development of existing areas.

As the ink dried, Adams leaned back in his chair, a sense of accomplishment washing over him. The opinion piece, though bold and against the prevailing sentiment, felt like an authentic expression of his convictions.

Later that day, Adams summoned his secretary to discuss the distribution of the article to prominent newspapers across the country.

"Mr. President, this is quite a departure from the usual discourse on expansion. Are you sure about this?"

Adams, his gaze steady, responded with conviction, "It's time for the nation to engage in a meaningful dialogue about our future. This article will be my contribution to that conversation."

The opinion penned by President John Quincy Adams made its way into newspapers across America. The response was immediate and fervent. The article, though met with criticism from proponents of Manifest Destiny, sparked a national conversation about the direction the young Republic should take.

Adams, undeterred by the backlash, stood by his convictions. He saw this as an opportunity to foster intellectual discourse, to challenge the status quo, and to guide the nation toward a future that embraced thoughtful expansion rather than unbridled conquest.

In the quiet corridors of the President's home, Adams had set in motion a dialogue that would shape the narrative of America's destiny in the years to come.

***

A Vision for America's Future

By John Quincy Adams, President of the United States

In contemplating the course of our young Republic, it becomes imperative to engage in a candid discussion about our national trajectory. The prevailing sentiment of constant westward expansion has been a defining aspect of our identity, yet it is my duty as your President to challenge this narrative and present an alternative vision for America's future.

For decades, we have pushed the frontier further west, fueled by the fervor of Manifest Destiny. While this ambition has shaped our nation's character, it is time to reassess our priorities and consider the consequences of unbridled growth. The West, once a vast expanse of opportunity, is now dotted with thriving settlements and cities, and it behooves us to turn our attention to nurturing and developing what we already possess.

This is not a rejection of progress but a call for thoughtful expansion. We must redirect our focus to the consolidation and cultivation of our existing territories, fostering prosperity and stability in regions that have borne witness to the struggles and triumphs of our people.

The notion of Manifest Destiny, while inspiring, must evolve to reflect the changing needs of our Republic. We are no longer a fledgling nation carving a path through the wilderness. We are a maturing society, and our approach to expansion should reflect our commitment to responsible governance and the well-being of our citizens.

It is essential to recognize that the unrelenting push westward has consequences. It strains our resources, exacerbates tensions with Indigenous populations, and spreads our population thin, hindering the development of cohesive communities. By turning our attention to the territories we already inhabit, we can ensure the prosperity of our citizens and the longevity of our great experiment in democracy.

This perspective is not one of retreat but of strategic foresight. It is a call to embrace the challenges of thoughtful expansion, to invest in the growth and prosperity of our existing territories, and to forge a nation that stands as a beacon of stability and enlightenment.

I understand that this vision may challenge deeply ingrained beliefs, but it is my duty as President to present a vision that serves the best interests of the American people. Let us engage in a national dialogue about the future we envision for our Republic, a future that balances ambition with responsibility, expansion with consolidation, and progress with stability.

John Quincy Adams

President of the United States

***

The early morning sun painted a warm glow over the bustling scene at the Nashville Inn. Andrew Jackson sat at a corner table; his breakfast spread before him. The aroma of freshly brewed coffee mingled with the clatter of plates and the hum of conversation, creating a lively atmosphere.

As Jackson perused the pages of the local newspaper, his eyes fixed on a particular article that bore the unmistakable mark of his political rival. The headline, "A Vision for America's Future," hinted at a departure from the prevailing sentiment of westward expansion.

Jackson's campaign manager approached the table, sensing the change in the air.

"Morning, General. What's caught your eye in the papers today?"

Jackson, his brow furrowed, slid the newspaper across the table. "Take a look at this, Francis. Adams is proposing a different vision for the country—a vision that's contrary to our stance on westward expansion."

Williamson scanned the article, his eyes narrowing. "It seems like Adams is calling for a different approach, consolidating what we have rather than charging into the unknown. Bold move, considering the prevailing sentiment."

Jackson, a fervent advocate for Western expansion, drummed his fingers on the table. "It's a calculated move, no doubt. But we can't let him shape the narrative unchallenged. Our stance on expansion is one of the pillars of our campaign."

Williamson nodded in agreement. "Perhaps we should consider crafting a response that reiterates the importance of pushing the frontier, of Manifest Destiny, and the opportunities it presents for our nation."

Jackson's eyes gleamed with determination. "You're right, Francis. We won't let Adams define our vision for America. We'll write an op-ed that speaks to the hearts of the people, which rallies them behind the idea of a boundless, expanding nation."

Later that day, the two men retired to a quiet corner of the Nashville Inn, surrounded by the hustle and bustle of patrons going about their day. Armed with quill and parchment, they set to work crafting a response—a passionate reaffirmation of their commitment to Western expansion.

The words flowed, each sentence carefully constructed to convey the essence of their belief in a nation that reached ever westward, embracing the challenges and opportunities that lay beyond the horizon.

"General, this article is strong. It captures the spirit of our campaign and counters Adams's narrative effectively."

Jackson, his steely gaze fixed on the written words, nodded approvingly. "We'll get this published in newspapers across the country. Let the people know that we stand firm in our conviction that America's destiny lies in the vast expanse of the West."

The op-ed, a rallying cry for Manifest Destiny and the unyielding spirit of expansion was dispatched to newspapers far and wide. It would soon find its way into the hands of Americans from the bustling cities to the remote frontier, shaping the discourse and fueling the fervor of a nation on the brink of a transformative election. The Nashville Inn, witness to this pivotal moment, buzzed with the energy of political determination as Jackson and his campaign manager set the stage for a clash of ideologies that would echo through the halls of history.

***

A Nation's Destiny Unfurls Westward

By Andrew Jackson

In the tapestry of our nation's history, woven with the threads of ambition and tenacity, one unassailable truth stands: the destiny of America unfurls westward. As we find ourselves at the cusp of a new era, we must reiterate our commitment to the principles that have defined our great Republic.

The call of the frontier, the promise of new opportunities, and the boundless possibilities that lie beyond the horizon have long stirred the hearts of Americans. It is a call that resonates with the spirit of Manifest Destiny—a spirit that propels us to expand, explore, and embrace the challenges that come with forging a nation in the crucible of the unknown.

While some may advocate for a more measured approach, suggesting that we consolidate our existing territories, I stand firm in my belief that the heart of

America beats in the untamed wilderness of the West. Our commitment to Western expansion is not just a policy; it is a proclamation of our faith in the inherent potential of our citizens and the resilience of our young Republic.

The West is not an obstacle to be overcome; it is an opportunity to be seized. It is a canvas upon which we paint the dreams and aspirations of generations to come. The pioneers who venture into the unknown, the settlers who build communities from the ground up, and the trailblazers who forge paths through uncharted territory—they embody the very essence of the American spirit.

As we look to the West, we see not just a geographical expanse but a frontier of promise and prosperity. It is a frontier that beckons us to cultivate, to build, and to mold the destiny of our nation. To turn away from the West is to deny the very nature of who we are—a people driven by the pursuit of something greater, something beyond the known.

The challenges that accompany western expansion are not to be feared but embraced. They are the crucible in which our mettle as a nation is tested and proven. It is in overcoming these challenges that we forge an identity as a resilient, united people.

In the coming years, as we chart our course forward, let us stand united in our commitment to western expansion. Let us reject the notion of limitations and embrace the vastness of the frontier with open hearts and unyielding determination. For in the West, we find not just the promise of a better tomorrow but the very essence of what it means to be American.

Andrew Jackson

Advocate for Manifest Destiny

Defender of America's Westward Spirit

***

A Call for Fairness and Economic Balance

By Andrew Jackson

In the halls of power, decisions are made that ripple through the fabric of our society. It is with deep concern for the welfare of our citizens that I address the recent enactment of the tariffs, an ill-conceived policy that threatens the very foundation of economic fairness in our great nation.

Let me be clear: tariffs, when applied judiciously, can serve as a legitimate tool for protecting domestic industries. However, the recent legislation dubbed the "Tariffs of Abomination," far exceeds the bounds of reasonable economic policy. Its implications weigh heavily on the shoulders of everyday Americans, and I must bring attention to the injustice embedded within these tariffs.

At the heart of this matter lies a fundamental question of fairness. The burden of these tariffs falls disproportionately on the shoulders of the Southern states, particularly those engaged in agriculture. As we well know, the South has long been an engine of economic prosperity, contributing significantly to the growth of our young Republic. Yet, with these tariffs, we find ourselves shackled by the weight of an economic policy that seems more punitive than protective.

The consequences are stark. southern farmers, already grappling with the challenges of fluctuating markets and unpredictable weather, now face an additional hurdle in the form of exorbitant tariffs on essential goods. This not only hampers their ability to compete in a global market but also threatens the very livelihoods of those who toil on the land to feed our nation.

Moreover, the tariffs have strained the delicate fabric of our union. It has sown seeds of discord between the regions, threatening the unity that our Founding Fathers worked tirelessly to achieve. A nation divided cannot endure, and it is incumbent upon us to rectify this course before irreparable damage is done.

I propose a reevaluation of these tariffs, and a reconsideration of their impact on the lives of our citizens. It is not a call for the abandonment of protective measures but a plea for a balanced and equitable approach. We must strive for policies that promote economic growth without unduly burdening any particular region.

In the spirit of unity and fairness, let us come together to rectify this grievous misstep. Our nation deserves policies that uplift all its citizens, which recognize the inherent strength found in the diversity of our states. Only through a commitment to fairness and economic balance can we ensure the continued prosperity and well-being of the American people.

Andrew Jackson

Advocate for Economic Fairness

Defender of the Union

***

A Vision for Economic Prosperity and National Growth

By John Quincy Adams

In the intricate dance of governance, decisions must be made with an eye toward the future, a future that demands not just economic stability but the enduring strength of our young Republic. It is in this context that I find it necessary to defend the tariffs recently passed by Congress—a policy that, while facing criticism, holds the promise of fostering economic growth and fortifying the foundations of our nation.

The tariffs in question have been met with skepticism and concern. However, it is crucial to view them not as impediments but as instruments of strategic economic planning. These tariffs aim to protect and nurture our fledgling industries, paving the way for a self-sufficient and robust American economy.

One must recognize the broader context within which these tariffs are enacted. Our nation is at a crossroads, with the echoes of the War of 1812 still resonating. To safeguard against economic vulnerabilities that could compromise our national security, we must cultivate and protect our industries from unfair competition.

While expressing apprehension, the southern states must understand that the intent is not punitive but protective. By incentivizing the growth of domestic industries, we lay the groundwork for a diverse and resilient economy. It is a vision that extends beyond sectional interests, aiming for the collective strength of the Union.

Critics argue that these tariffs disproportionately affect southern farmers, placing an undue burden on their shoulders. However, it is imperative to recognize that the policy is a comprehensive approach to economic development. While challenges may arise in the short term, the long-term benefits include a flourishing national economy that transcends regional boundaries.

Furthermore, the revenue generated from these tariffs can be reinvested in infrastructure, education, and technological advancements, propelling our nation into a new era of progress. We must not shy away from temporary sacrifices if they pave the way for a brighter and more prosperous future for all.

In conclusion, the tariffs of 1828 are not a haphazard imposition but a calculated step toward securing the economic vitality of our great nation. As we weather the challenges of the present, let us remain steadfast in our commitment to a vision that transcends sectional interests—a vision that places the United States at the forefront of global economic leadership.

John Quincy Adams

Architect of Economic Prosperity

Champion of the American Future

***

Unmasking the Corrupt Bargain - An Affront to Democracy

By Andrew Jackson

In the hallowed halls of our nation's history, a specter of corruption looms—a dark chapter that threatens the very foundation of our democratic principles. The 1824 election, hailed as a beacon of participatory governance, has been tarnished by a shadowy alliance, a corrupt bargain that betrayed the will of the people and propelled John Quincy Adams into the presidency.

Let us cast aside the veils of political rhetoric and address the glaring truth that stains the legacy of our electoral system. In 1824, the voice of the American people was silenced, their choice overridden by a behind-the-scenes arrangement orchestrated by none other than John Adams and Henry Clay.

The evidence is glaring after a hotly contested election in which no candidate secured a majority in the Electoral College, the decision fell to the House of Representatives. It is here that the whispers of a nefarious pact between Adams and Clay materialized into a reality that forever altered the course of our nation.

Henry Clay, wielding considerable influence as the Speaker of the House, threw his support behind Adams. In return, Adams appointed Clay as his Secretary of State. The very office that had served as a steppingstone to the presidency for many before. This, my fellow citizens, is the definition of a corrupt bargain—an underhanded exchange that subverted the will of the people.

The implications are profound. The presidency, intended to be a reflection of the people's choice, became a pawn in the hands of a political elite more concerned with self-interest than the democratic ideals upon which this nation was founded.

We must not forget the outcry of the people, the anger that simmered as the true nature of this backroom deal became apparent. The trust in the democratic process was betrayed, and the seeds of disillusionment were sown.

This is not an accusation made lightly. It is a call to arms for every citizen who cherishes the principles of democracy. Our nation deserves leaders who ascend to power through the genuine will of the people, not through clandestine agreements that subvert the very essence of our electoral system.

As we stand on the precipice of a new era, let us remember the lessons of 1824. Let us demand transparency, accountability, and a restoration of the democratic ideals that should guide the course of our Republic.

Andrew Jackson

Defender of Democratic Principles

Voice of the American People

**"

Upholding Integrity and Dispelling Unfounded Claims

By John Quincy Adams, President of the United States

In the theater of democracy, the accusation of corruption is a grave charge that must not be taken lightly. Recent claims suggesting a corrupt bargain between myself and the esteemed Henry Clay to secure the presidency in 1824 are not only baseless but a disservice to the principles that underpin our great nation.

Let me be unequivocal: there was no corrupt bargain. The process that unfolded in the aftermath of the

1824 election adhered strictly to the constitutional provisions in place. The House of Representatives, charged with deciding the outcome when no candidate secured a majority, fulfilled its duty with integrity and fidelity to the democratic ideals we hold dear.

The insinuation that a nefarious pact existed between Mr. Clay and me is a distortion of the truth. Henry Clay, a man of unwavering principles and a dedicated public servant, made a conscious decision to support my candidacy based on shared beliefs and a vision for the future of our nation. The subsequent appointment as Secretary of State was not a reward for political maneuvering but a recognition of his statesmanship and qualifications for the role.

As the head of this great Republic, my commitment to transparency, accountability, and the principle of democracy remains steadfast. I entered the presidency with a singular focus: to serve the American people to the best of my ability and by the constitutionally prescribed processes.

The presidency is not a prize to be bartered but a sacred trust to be earned through dedication, service, and the will of the people. To impugn the legitimacy of the 1824 election is to undermine the very foundation of our democratic system—a system that has withstood the test of time and served as a beacon of governance for the world.

In the spirit of civic responsibility, I hope we can rise above baseless accusations and engage in a discourse that focuses on the pressing issues facing our nation. The challenges are great, and our collective efforts are needed to address them with the gravity they deserve.

As we move forward, let us remain vigilant in safeguarding the integrity of our democratic processes, respecting the decisions made within the bounds of the Constitution, and upholding the principles that bind us together as one nation, indivisible.

John Quincy Adams

President of the United States

Guardian of Democratic Ideals

***

In the Spirit of Jeffersonian Principles

By John Quincy Adams, President of the United States

In the corridors of history, the influence of Thomas Jefferson looms large—a guiding light whose principles continue to shape the destiny of our young Republic. As we stand on the threshold of the 1828 election, I am compelled to articulate why I believe, in the spirit of Jeffersonian ideals, he would find alignment with the principles and policies of my administration.

Thomas Jefferson, the author of the Declaration of Independence and a staunch advocate for individual liberties and the pursuit of happiness, envisioned a nation that embraced the diversity of its citizenry. He championed an agrarian society where the yeoman farmer played a vital role, and the virtues of simplicity and self-sufficiency were extolled.

In my presidency, I have sought to uphold these very principles. I have championed the cause of internal improvements to connect the vast expanse of our nation, ensuring that the benefits of progress reach every corner. The vision of a self-sufficient America, resilient in the face of challenges, aligns with Jefferson's call for an agrarian democracy.

Moreover, Jefferson believed in the diffusion of power, a sentiment expressed in his famous quote, "The government is best which governs least." Throughout my term, I have worked diligently to preserve the delicate balance between federal authority and state sovereignty, striving to empower the states and safeguard the liberties of our citizens.

On matters of foreign policy, I have endeavored to maintain a policy of neutrality and non-intervention, echoing Jefferson's call for a nation at peace with the world. The pursuit of diplomatic solutions and the avoidance of unnecessary entanglements reflect a commitment to Jefferson's vision of a republic free from the shackles of unnecessary conflicts.

While Jefferson and I may have differences in approach, I believe that the underlying principles of limited government, individual liberties, and an agrarian society find resonance in the policies of my administration. As we navigate the complex landscape of the 1828 election, it is my sincere hope that voters consider the alignment between Jeffersonian ideals and the path my presidency has charted for our beloved nation.

In the spirit of democracy, let us engage in a robust and principled discourse, honoring the legacy of Thomas Jefferson and striving toward a future that reflects the enduring principles upon which our great Republic was founded.

John Quincy Adams

President of the United States

Steward of Jeffersonian Principles

***

A Call to Uphold Jeffersonian Ideals

By Andrew Jackson

As the 1828 election approaches, it is crucial to reflect on the principles that define our nation and the visionary leadership of Thomas Jefferson. I believe, with unwavering conviction, that the spirit of Jeffersonian ideals finds a home in the vision I offer for America's future.

Thomas Jefferson, an architect of liberty and a champion of individual freedoms, envisioned a government that derived its power from the people—an institution that served the common man and protected his rights. In my campaign for the presidency, I carry the torch of this noble vision, committed to a government that is of the people, by the people, and for the people.

Jefferson believed in the sovereignty of states, the empowerment of local communities, and the preservation of individual liberties against the encroachment of centralized authority. I share this belief wholeheartedly. Throughout my career, I have championed the cause of states' rights, advocating for the autonomy of individual states to shape their destinies free from undue federal interference.

Furthermore, Jefferson was a proponent of agrarian democracy, recognizing the vital role of the yeoman farmer in fostering the nation's prosperity. In this spirit, I stand as a tireless advocate for the interests of the common man, seeking to ensure that the benefits of our nation's growth are distributed equitably, and that the foundations of our economy remain rooted in the strength of the American farmer.

Jefferson's commitment to a restrained and fiscally responsible government is a principle I hold dear. I am dedicated to curbing government excesses, eliminating wasteful spending, and ensuring that the hard-earned resources of our citizens are used judiciously for the betterment of our nation.

As we approach this pivotal election, let us honor the legacy of Thomas Jefferson by embracing the principles that defined his leadership. A commitment to individual liberties, states' rights, and fiscal responsibility should guide our choices as citizens. It is my earnest belief that, in upholding these Jeffersonian ideals, we pave the way for a future that honors the vision of our Founding Fathers.

In the spirit of democracy, let us unite under the banner of principles that transcend partisan divides, working toward a future that reflects the timeless ideals upon which our great Republic was built.

Andrew Jackson

Advocate for Jeffersonian Principles

Champion of the Common Man

Chapter 12

Voting Begins

October 31, 1828

As dawn painted streaks of pink and gold across the Pennsylvania sky, Jonathan Turner, a hardworking farmer, rose with the roosters, ready to fulfill his civic duty. The air was crisp, carrying the promise of a clear autumn day, as Jonathan donned his worn-out coat and made his way to the bustling heart of his small town.

The sturdy brick town hall stood as a symbol of democracy; its doors thrown open to welcome citizens like Jonathan who were eager to cast their votes in the presidential election. The excitement in the air was palpable, a tangible energy that pulsed through the community.

As Jonathan approached the hall, he exchanged nods and greetings with his neighbors, recognizing familiar faces in the growing crowd. The town, once quiet in the early morning hours, now buzzed with anticipation and spirited conversations about the future of the nation.

Inside the hall, wooden booths were set up for each voter, providing a private space to make their choice. The scent of ink and paper permeated the air as Jonathan stepped into one of the booths, holding the folded ballot in his calloused hands. The parchment bore the names of two distinguished candidates: John Quincy Adams and Andrew Jackson.

In the quiet of the booth, Jonathan reflected on the principles he held dear. His worn fingers traced over the names on the ballot, contemplating the vision each candidate presented for the young Republic. The decision weighed heavily on him, a responsibility he took seriously.

After careful consideration, Jonathan marked his choice, folded the ballot, and approached the ballot box. The rhythmic clink of the wooden box echoed through the hall as he dropped his vote into its depths, sealing his contribution to the democratic process.

Exiting the town hall, Jonathan felt a sense of pride and duty. The act of casting his vote wasn't just a civic obligation; it was a testament to the power of the people to shape the destiny of their nation. As he walked back to his farm, the sun rising higher in the sky, Jonathan Turner carried with him the hope that his voice, along with those of countless others, would resonate in the outcome of the 1828 election.

***

In the heart of Columbus, Ohio, a bustling city that echoed the growing fervor of the young United States, James Anderson closed the door of his workshop as the clock struck 1:00 in the afternoon on October 31st, 1828. With a sense of purpose, he set off towards City Hall, a sturdy building that stood as a bastion of civic engagement.

The streets of Columbus were alive with the rhythm of daily life, horse-drawn carriages clattering along cobblestone roads and pedestrians weaving through the midday bustle. As James made his way through the city, he couldn't escape the palpable energy that hung in the air—a shared anticipation of the presidential election.

Arriving at City Hall, James found himself amidst a diverse crowd of fellow citizens. Businessmen in fine suits, laborers in worn overalls, and women adorned in modest dresses—all converging on this central hub to exercise the right to vote. The democratic spirit of the nation thrived within these walls.

Inside the building, James joined the line leading to the voting booths. Conversations hummed around him, snippets of discussions about the merits of the candidates and the future of the nation. As he approached the booth, he felt a mixture of excitement and solemnity, aware that his vote held significance in the broader tapestry of democracy.

With the ballot in hand, James carefully considered the choices before him. The names of Adams and Jackson stared back, each representing a distinct vision for the country. In the quiet of the booth, he reflected on his beliefs, the values he held dear, and the aspirations he had for the nation's future.

As the quill scratched against the parchment, marking his choice, James felt a surge of pride. This act, seemingly small in the grand scheme, carried the weight of democratic ideals—a tangible expression of his voice in the shaping of the nation's destiny.

Exiting the booth, James dropped his ballot into the wooden box, the soft thud echoing through the hall. The satisfaction of participating in the democratic process lingered as he left City Hall, the sun casting long shadows across the streets of Columbus.

***

On the crisp afternoon of November 7th, 1828, the air at Andrew Jackson's sprawling plantation outside Nashville carried a subtle anticipation. The day cast long shadows over the estate, and the rustle of leaves hinted at the changing season. Dressed in a well-worn suit, Jackson emerged from the imposing mansion, his gait purposeful as he headed towards the awaiting carriage.

"Mr. Jackson, everything's prepared for your journey to the church," called out one of the estate workers, tipping his hat respectfully.

"Thank you," replied Jackson, his weathered features breaking into a determined smile. Today was not just any day; it was Election Day, the culmination of a fierce campaign that had gripped the nation. As he settled into the carriage, he couldn't shake the gravity of the moment—the culmination of years of service, sacrifice, and the relentless pursuit of the highest office in the land.

The carriage creaked into motion, winding its way down the tree-lined path. The Hermitage seemed to resonate with the weight of history on this particular afternoon. As they approached the local church, the energy of the election season permeated the air.

Upon arrival, Jackson was met with a congregation of neighbors, farmers, and townsfolk. The church, with its white steeple piercing the sky, echoed with the murmur of conversations and the shuffling of feet. The scent of autumn lingered, a reminder that change was not only in the air but also on the ballots.

Entering the church, Jackson navigated through the maze of pews towards the voting booths. The act of casting a vote for oneself might seem routine, but for the old warrior-statesman, it carried profound significance. As he marked the ballot bearing his name, he couldn't help but reflect on the journey that had brought him to this point—the battles fought, the sacrifices made, and the unwavering belief in the principles that fueled his pursuit.

A fellow parishioner, recognizing Jackson, offered a nod of respect. "Best of luck, General," he said, a sentiment echoed by others in the room.

"Thank you, my friend," Jackson replied, his gaze unwavering. Leaving the church, he felt a mixture of pride and humility. The die was cast, and the fate of the nation rested in the hands of its citizens.

As the carriage rolled back towards the Hermitage, Jackson's thoughts turned to the countless individuals who had exercised their right to vote during this consequential election. The journey back up the estate's path was a quiet reflection, a moment for the old warrior to consider the weight of the democratic process, the hopes of a nation, and the possibilities ahead.

The evening dipped below the horizon, casting the Hermitage in a warm glow as Jackson, having fulfilled his duty as a citizen, returned to his home—a home that, for a brief moment, stood as a beacon in the young Republic, awaiting the unfolding of history.

***

As the brisk morning of November 9th, 1828, unfolded in the quiet town of Quincy, Massachusetts, the air crackled with a sense of civic duty. John Quincy Adams, accompanied by his wife, Louisa Catherine, emerged from their modest home, the Peacefield, to participate in a ritual that was both a privilege and a responsibility—voting in the election.

Having arrived from Washington City the evening before, the couple navigated the familiar paths toward the town hall, the heart of their community's democratic engagement. The town, nestled between rolling hills and adorned with colonial architecture, exuded a timeless charm that mirrored the endurance of American democracy.

"John, it's a beautiful morning," remarked Louisa Catherine, her eyes scanning the quaint surroundings as they strolled together.

"Indeed, my dear. A day of immense importance," replied John Quincy, his gaze fixed on the horizon. The journey from the nation's capital to this small enclave carried the weight of a campaign that had traversed the vast expanse of the United States.

Arriving at the town hall, they were met with the bustling activity of fellow citizens—farmers, merchants, and laborers—each with their convictions and aspirations for the nation. The town hall stood as a testament to the enduring spirit of American governance.

Inside, the familiar scent of ink and parchment greeted them. The voting booths, separated by worn curtains, held the promise of a silent proclamation of one's allegiance. The names on the ballot embodied the competing visions for the future.

John Quincy, with Louisa by his side, approached the booths. The atmosphere inside the hall was hushed, the gravity of the moment palpable. The quill met the parchment, and for a fleeting moment, the president was just a citizen expressing his choice, even if that choice happened to be for himself.

"John, it's a privilege to cast our vote in this manner," whispered Louisa as she looked down at his ballot in his hands.

"It is, indeed, my love. A cornerstone of our democracy," he replied, his voice carrying a mix of gratitude and determination.

Exiting the booth, they joined the line to deposit their ballots into the wooden box. A neighbor nodded in acknowledgment, recognizing the statesman in their midst. The act of voting connected them to their fellow citizens, transcending the distinctions of class or office.

As they stepped back into the crisp autumn air, John Quincy and Louisa Catherine exchanged a glance that spoke volumes—a shared acknowledgment of the significance of this democratic tradition. The town hall, with its echoing footsteps and murmured conversations, bore witness to a moment in time when a president, now a private citizen, participated in a process that symbolized the essence of the American experiment.

***

In the rugged mountains near Asheville, North Carolina, where the air carried the scent of pine and the sounds of nature echoed through the valleys, lived Tobias Miller. His humble cabin, nestled against the backdrop of majestic peaks, served as a testament to a life intimately connected with the land. On the morning of November 14th, Tobias prepared for a journey that would take him and his two sons down to town to cast his vote in the election.

"Boys, gather 'round," Tobias called, his deep voice resonating through the rustic dwelling. His two sons, Elijah and Samuel, emerged from their morning chores, curiosity etched on their young faces.

"We're heading down to town to vote today," Tobias announced, a glint of pride in his eyes. "It's a right and a duty we hold dear."

The trio set off on foot, following a well-worn trail that wound its way through the dense forest. The crisp November air carried a sense of purpose, and the crunch of leaves underfoot served as a prelude to the democratic ritual awaiting them in town.

As they descended from the mountains, the landscape transformed into a panorama of rolling hills and meandering streams. The town, a modest collection of buildings, came into view—a haven where mountain folk gathered to exchange news, barter goods, and, on this particular day, participate in the democratic process.

Arriving at the town tavern, a hub of community activity, Tobias and his sons found a gathering of neighbors engaged in spirited conversations about the candidates. The air buzzed with opinions, creating an atmosphere that mirrored the diversity of voices in the young Republic.

Inside the tavern, a makeshift polling station had been set up. A wooden booth with a tattered curtain offered a semblance of privacy for voters to mark their ballots. Tobias, standing tall in his weathered boots, entered the booth with a sense of solemnity, his sons observing the process with wide-eyed fascination.

The ballot, bearing the names of the candidates, represented the crossroads of a nation grappling with its identity. Tobias, with a steadiness earned from years of hard living, marked his choice for the candidate he believed would champion the interests of the common man.

Exiting the booth, Tobias dropped his ballot into the wooden box, the hollow thud echoing through the tavern. As he turned to leave, he caught sight of his sons, their gazes fixed on him with a mixture of admiration and understanding.

"Today, boys," Tobias said, placing a hand on each of their shoulders, "we've played a part in shaping the course of this great land."

The journey back to their mountain cabin was filled with a quiet satisfaction. The mountains, ever steadfast, bore witness to the passage of generations and the ebb and flow of the democratic tide. Tobias, Elijah, and Samuel, having left their mark on the ballot box, carried with them the knowledge that, in a young nation's journey, every vote mattered—a ripple in the vast river of American democracy.

Chapter 13

The People's President

November 17, 1828

In the grandeur of the Executive Mansion, John Quincy Adams felt the weight of history pressing upon him. The morning dawned with a sense of anticipation, and as Adams walked through the opulent halls of the presidential residence, the news reached him like a gust of frigid wind — he had lost the popular vote in the election.

His trusted secretary, a somber expression etched on his face, approached Adams with a sealed envelope. "Mr. President, the latest reports have arrived," he said, handing over the missive.

Adams broke the seal stoically and unfolded the contents. His eyes scanned the words that bore the truth he had been bracing for. The popular vote had tilted away from him, a fact that carried a weight beyond mere statistics.

A heavy silence hung in the room as Adams absorbed the reality before him. The echoes of a contentious campaign reverberated in his mind — the debates, the accusations, and the fervor that had defined the political landscape. Now, the popular vote stood as a measure of the public sentiment, and the outcome was a resounding verdict.

Turning to his secretary, Adams spoke with a composed but reflective tone, "Democracy has spoken, and we must heed its voice. I must respect the will of the people."

As news of the popular vote loss spread within the Executive Mansion, an air of contemplation settled over the residence. advisors and staff moved with measured steps, understanding the historical significance of the moment. The mansion, adorned with the symbols of the nation's past and aspirations for the future, became a sanctuary for reflection.

Later in the day, Adams gathered with a few close advisors in the East Room. "This is a pivotal moment," he remarked, his gaze fixed on the expansive grounds visible through the large windows. "The people have spoken, and the democratic process marches forward."

In the corridors of power, where decisions shaped the destiny of the United States, Adams confronted the ebb and flow of political tides. The loss in the popular vote, a poignant chapter in his storied career, became a testament to the enduring strength of the American democratic experiment.

***

The morning cast a golden hue over the hills surrounding the Hermitage. The sprawling estate, usually steeped in the tranquility of the Southern landscape, witnessed a rare sense of urgency on the morning of November 18th, 1828.

As the rustle of leaves echoed through the oak trees, a lone rider emerged on the horizon, kicking up dust on the dirt path leading to the mansion. The messenger, adorned in a weathered coat and clutching a sealed envelope, urged his steed forward with determination. The news he carried bore the weight of the nation's democratic will.

Upon reaching the doors of the mansion, the rider dismounted, his boots meeting the gravel with a hurried determination. The estate's caretaker, a seasoned hand familiar with the rhythms of the plantation, greeted him.

"I need to see General Jackson. It's urgent," declared the messenger, his breath visible in the cool morning air.

The caretaker, sensing the gravity of the situation, guided the messenger towards the mansion, where Jackson's trusted aide waited on the porch.

"General Jackson's in the study. This way," the aide said, leading the messenger through the grand foyer adorned with portraits and mementos of battles fought.

In the study, Jackson, a figure of military prowess and political resilience, sat at his desk, surrounded by maps and documents. The messenger entered, his presence breaking the stillness of the room.

"General Jackson, sir," the messenger began, catching his breath. "I bring news from Nashville."

Jackson, his piercing blue eyes fixing on the messenger, gestured for him to proceed. The room, filled with the fragrance of polished wood and the soft crackle of the fireplace, seemed to hold its breath.

"You've won the popular vote, sir. The people have spoken, and their voice is clear," the messenger conveyed, handing over the sealed envelope containing the official confirmation.

For a moment, silence hung in the room like a suspended chord. Then, a slow smile crept across Jackson's weathered face, lines etched by years of service to his country. The weight of a nation's trust, expressed through the ballot, resonated in that fleeting silence.

"Thank you," Jackson finally uttered, his voice carrying a mix of humility and gratitude. "This victory belongs to the people. It's a testament to their belief in a vision for this nation."

Word of the news spread. Jackson's aides and servants, catching wind of the victory, exchanged congratulatory nods. The estate, so often a witness to the ebb and flow of history, now stood as a haven of triumph.

As the messenger prepared to leave, Jackson stood and extended a firm handshake. "Tell the good people of Nashville that their support humbles me. We're bound by the shared spirit of democracy, and together, we'll continue the journey that lies ahead."

The messenger, his duty fulfilled, mounted his horse once more, leaving the mansion behind. In his wake, the estate basked in the warmth of a newfound victory, as Jackson, a man of the people, prepared to carry their aspirations into the unfolding chapters of the nation's history.

***

The news of Andrew Jackson's triumph in the popular vote rippled through the vibrant streets of Nashville like wildfire on the morning of November 18th, 1828. The air, already infused with the spirit of anticipation, crackled with an electrifying energy that echoed through every alley and avenue.

As word spread, jubilant residents spilled out of homes and shops, their faces aglow with excitement. Flags adorned with stars and stripes fluttered from storefronts, and the rhythmic beat of drums filled the air. The people of Nashville, proud of their native son, embraced the victory with unrestrained enthusiasm.

In the town square, a gathering of citizens transformed into a spontaneous celebration. Musicians tuned their instruments, and the lively notes of fiddles and banjos echoed against the brick facades. Dancers twirled in rhythmic patterns, their exuberant movements reflecting the joy that pulsed through the crowd.

A local tavern, known for lively discussions and spirited toasts, became a focal point of the revelry. The clinking of glasses and hearty cheers resonated within its walls as patrons raised a toast to Jackson's success.

On the steps of the courthouse, a charismatic orator swept up in the fervor of the moment addressed the growing assembly. "Fellow Nashvillians, today we celebrate not just a victory for our native son but a victory for the very essence of democracy! Andrew Jackson, a Tennessean through and through, has triumphed in the popular vote. This victory is a testament to the power of the people's voice!"

The crowd erupted in cheers, hats tossed into the air, and laughter mingled with the lively tunes. The streets, now alive with a kaleidoscope of colors from banners and ribbons, bore witness to a spectacle of unity and pride.

In the market square, vendors peddled their wares amid the festivities. Baskets of fresh produce, handmade crafts, and trinkets exchanged hands as the celebration transformed the normally bustling marketplace into a carnival of joy.

As the day unfolded, the celebrations continued to cascade through the neighborhoods of Nashville. Families gathered on porches, sharing tales of their connection to Jackson and relishing the shared sense of achievement. Children ran through the streets, waving miniature flags, caught up in the contagious spirit of celebration.

In the glow of the Tennessee sun, Nashville became a canvas painted with the exuberance of democracy in action. Jackson, the local hero, had resonated with the people, and his victory in the popular vote became a shared triumph for every citizen who called Nashville home. The streets echoed with the refrain of a community united, and the celebration, like the legacy of Jackson himself, etched its mark on the heart of the vibrant city.

The morning bathed Nashville in a warm glow as Andrew Jackson, the newly elected president, entered the bustling inn on November 19th, 1828. Accompanied by his loyal campaign manager and now Vice President-elect, the esteemed John Calhoun, the trio sought refuge in a corner of the bustling establishment to discuss the election results and the path forward.

Seated at a well-worn wooden table, Jackson's piercing blue eyes scanned the room, acknowledging the nods and cheers from well-wishers, their faces radiant with excitement, and approached the president-elect to offer heartfelt congratulations. Jackson, never one to shy away from connecting with the people, exchanged warm greetings and hearty handshakes, gratitude etched across his features.

As the trio settled into their private enclave, the air crackling with the hum of celebration, Senator Martin Van Buren, who had arrived the evening before, couldn't help but smile. "General," he began, a twinkle in his eye, "you've done it. The people have spoken, and their voice is a resounding affirmation of your leadership."

Jackson, a man of few words but profound convictions, nodded in acknowledgment. His campaign manager who had played a pivotal role in orchestrating the triumph, continued, "We've made history, sir. The people see in you a leader who understands their struggles and aspirations."

The discussion delved into the intricacies of the election results, the states won, and the challenges ahead. Jackson, though relishing the victory, maintained a pragmatic focus on the responsibilities that lay ahead as the steward of the nation.

Amidst the discourse, a server approached with a tray bearing glasses of Tennessee whiskey, a local elixir known for its robust flavor. The clinking of glasses signaled a pause in the conversation as Van Buren stood, raising his glass high.

"To Andrew Jackson, the people's president!" declared Van Buren, his voice carrying across the room.

A wave of applause and cheers erupted, drawing the attention of the inn's patrons. Jackson, a man of action rather than eloquence, acknowledged the toast with a humble nod. The sentiment, however, was not lost on him.

The celebration continued, and as the day unfolded, the Nashville Inn became a microcosm of the nation's exuberance. Jackson, surrounded by well-wishers and supporters, embodied the spirit of a people who had found a champion in their president.

The inn stood as a testament to the resilience of democracy. Andrew Jackson, the man of the people, had ascended to the highest office, and in that Nashville Inn, the celebration of his victory echoed the collective heartbeat of a nation ready for a new chapter.

Chapter 14

Corrupt Bargain Again

November 25, 1828

The morning cast a feeble light through the grand windows of the Executive Mansion, illuminating the expansive dining room. However, the atmosphere within was far from radiant. President Adams, his usually composed demeanor disrupted, sat at the head of the table with a furrowed brow and a heavy heart.

The headlines in the morning newspapers had brought a bitter reality to the forefront — Adams had lost the popular vote. The revelation stung, a bruise on the pride of a man who had long believed in the rectitude of his administration.

As Adams picked at his breakfast, his campaign manager entered the room. The air hung heavy with an unspoken tension as the president's sharp gaze met the weary countenance of his aide.

"Morning, Mr. President," the campaign manager greeted cautiously, noting the somber mood that permeated the room.

Adams, his usual eloquence momentarily silenced, merely nodded in acknowledgment.

The campaign manager approached the table, choosing his words carefully. "Sir, I know the news has been difficult to digest. Losing the vote was not the outcome we anticipated."

Adams, his jaw clenched, finally spoke with a measured intensity, "Difficult to digest is an understatement, James. The people have spoken, or rather, they have spoken against me, against everything I've strived to achieve."

James took a seat across from the president, his posture reflecting the moment's weight. "We faced a formidable opponent. Jackson's appeal to the common man resonated deeply, and the people responded."

Adams, pushing his plate away, leaned back in his chair, a brooding frustration evident in his eyes. "Resonated? More like manipulated. The man is a populist, a man of the people, they say. But what about the nuances and complexities of governance? The people have chosen charisma over competence."

The campaign manager, no stranger to navigating such tempestuous moments, chose his words carefully. "Mr. President, the electorate can be unpredictable. Perhaps it's time to recalibrate our approach. Reach out to the people, understand their concerns, and bridge the gap."

Adams, though receptive to the advice, found it hard to mask his discontent. "Recalibrate? James, this nation needs a leader who can see beyond the immediate desires of the people. We're not here to pander; we're here to guide, to lead with wisdom."

The campaign manager sighed, understanding the uphill battle they faced. "I share your sentiments, sir. But in the realm of politics, perception often shapes reality. We must adapt to the changing winds to weather this storm."

Adams, his frustration evident, stood abruptly, pacing the room. "Adapt, yes. But at what cost? To compromise principles for the sake of popularity? That's not leadership; that's capitulation."

Rising to join the president, James attempted to inject a note of pragmatism. "History is replete with leaders who faced adversity, adapted, and emerged stronger. We too can navigate these turbulent waters, sir."

Adams, his frustration manifesting in a weary sigh, acknowledged the truth in James' words. "Very well, James. We shall navigate, but not at the cost of our principles. The journey may be arduous, but we shall persevere."

As the day unfolded, the Executive Mansion echoed with the weight of reflection and adaptation.

President Adams, grappling with the reality of a changing political landscape, stood at a crossroads, unsure of the compromises he was willing to make. The newspapers may have carried the news of defeat, but the pages of history were yet to be written.

In the hushed corridors of power, behind closed doors, President Adams and his campaign manager engaged in a conversation that danced on the edge of political maneuvering. The specter of defeat in the popular vote loomed large, casting a shadow over the Adams administration's prospects for a favorable view from history.

"Mr. President," James began cautiously, choosing his words with precision, "we find ourselves in a challenging position. The popular vote has spoken, but we must not forget the intricacies of the electoral college."

Adams, his countenance still reflecting the disappointment from the morning's news, arched an eyebrow in contemplation. "Go on, James. I'm listening."

James took a deep breath before laying out a proposal that lingered on the fringes of political ethics. "There's a notion circulating, sir, that we explore the possibility of persuading Pennsylvania, New York, and Louisiana to reconsider their electoral college votes. If we can sway them, we might secure the presidency for a second term."

The gravity of the suggestion hung in the air. Adams studied his campaign manager with a measured intensity. "Are you suggesting we tamper with the electoral process? I may be many things, but I won't be a party to undermining the very foundations of our democracy."

James, aware of the delicate nature of his proposition, hastened to clarify. "Not tamper, Mr. President. Influence. It's a delicate dance, a strategic recalibration of alliances. We've seen such shifts in the past. If we can garner support from key electors, it could be a legitimate path forward."

Adams, his mind a battleground between ideals and pragmatism, leaned back in his chair. "Legitimate or not, James, it reeks of manipulation. We must tread carefully, for the sake of the office and the principles we hold dear."

The campaign manager, recognizing the weight of the moment, continued, "I understand your reservations, sir. However, consider the alternative. Jackson, a man with a populist appeal but lacking the nuanced understanding required for governance, assumes the highest office. Is that truly in the best interest of the nation?"

Adams, conflicted, ran his fingers through his graying hair. The weight of responsibility bore heavily on his shoulders. "Convince me, James. Convince me that this path, however treacherous, serves the greater good."

In a voice laden with conviction, James responded, "It's not about personal gain, Mr. President. It's about ensuring that the nation is guided by a steady hand, by someone who comprehends the complexities of leadership. A strategic shift in the electoral college may be the only way to safeguard the principles we hold dear."

As the two men continued their discussion, the room bore witness to the delicate dance of politics, where ideals and pragmatism collided in the pursuit of power. The road ahead remained uncertain, and the echoes of democracy reverberated in the corridors of decision-making, awaiting the final steps of a complex dance.

***

Deep within the corridors of power in Louisiana, a clandestine alliance formed, weaving a political tapestry that would reshape the course of the electoral college. The state's governor, a shrewd tactician with a keen understanding of the political currents, had long held an antipathy toward Andrew Jackson. A clandestine meeting, cloaked in secrecy, unfolded in the governor's office as the plan took shape.

The governor, a staunch opponent of Jackson, addressed a gathering of influential figures in the state legislature. "Gentlemen," he began, his voice a low, conspiratorial whisper, "we find ourselves at a crossroads. Jackson's victory in our state does not align with our vision for the future. We must consider alternatives."

The legislators, a mix of seasoned politicians and influential powerbrokers, exchanged furtive glances. Their allegiance, though rooted in personal and political interests, aligned with the governor's disdain for Jackson.

"We have the power to shape the electoral college vote," the governor continued, his eyes gleaming with determination. "Louisiana can become a linchpin in securing a second term for President Adams. But we must act swiftly and with precision."

The legislature, fueled by a collective desire to thwart Jackson's ascent, committed to forming a slate of electors sympathetic to Adams. The governor outlined a strategic plan to leverage the state's political machinery, ensuring the electors chosen would cast their votes for Adams when the time came.

One legislator, a seasoned political strategist, questioned the feasibility of such a covert operation. "Governor, what assurances do we have that this plan won't unravel? Jackson's supporters are fervent, and our actions could face scrutiny."

The governor, an expert tactician, unfolded a meticulous blueprint. "We control the narrative, gentlemen. Our actions must be veiled in the guise of protecting the interests of Louisiana. We frame it as a matter of principled governance, a safeguard against what we perceive as the potential dangers of a Jackson presidency."

The legislators, their reservations momentarily quelled, nodded in agreement. The plan, though fraught with risks, resonated with the shared disdain for Jackson's populist appeal.

The governor concluded the meeting with a sobering reminder. "This is a pivotal moment for Louisiana, for our values, and for the nation. Our decisions here will echo through history. We have the chance to be architects of destiny."

As the gathering dispersed, a cloak of secrecy enveloped the plan. The clandestine coalition, bound by a shared vision and political pragmatism, set in motion the machinery of influence. Louisiana, a key player in the unfolding drama, poised itself to alter the electoral landscape, leaving the fate of the presidency hanging in the balance.

***

In the heart of New York, a political chess game unfolded, its moves orchestrated by strategic minds and fueled by longstanding rivalries. The governor, a wily adversary of Martin Van Buren, viewed the impending electoral college vote as an opportunity to settle scores and shift the balance of power.

Governor William Stansbury, with his sharp political acumen and a history of clashes with Van Buren legendary, convened a closed-door meeting with a select group of legislators sympathetic to his cause.

The atmosphere in the room crackled with tension as the governor laid out his plan to alter the trajectory of New York's electoral votes.

"Gentlemen," Governor Stansbury began, his voice a low hum, "we find ourselves at the nexus of power and influence. Van Buren's sway in this state is a thorn in our side, and we have an opportunity to wield our influence to disrupt his plans."

The legislators, a mix of seasoned politicians and influential figures, listened intently. The governor continued, "Van Buren is Jackson's right-hand man, and we know how closely aligned their interests are. If we can tip the scales in favor of Adams, it would be a blow not only to Jackson but also to Van Buren's political machinations."

One legislator, a staunch ally of the governor, voiced a concern, "But how do we maneuver around the entrenched support for Jackson in our state? His popularity is not to be underestimated."

The governor, a shrewd tactician, leaned forward, his gaze unwavering. "We exploit the fault lines, my friends. There are fractures within the Democratic ranks. Van Buren's ambitions have made him enemies even within his party. We leverage those divisions to our advantage."

The plan, unveiled with meticulous detail, involved the legislature electing an alternate slate of electors who would pledge their allegiance to John Quincy Adams. The governor outlined a strategy to frame this move as a principled stand against what they portrayed as the potential dangers of a Jackson presidency.

As the meeting progressed, the legislators grappled with the audacity of the plan. The stakes were high, and the consequences of their actions weighed heavily on their minds. Yet, the allure of disrupting Van Buren's influence proved too enticing to resist.

One legislator, a fervent critic of Van Buren, spoke up, "This is our chance to send a message. To show that New York cannot be dictated by the whims of one man. It's time to break free from the shackles of Van Buren's control."

The room, charged with a sense of rebellion, collectively agreed to proceed with the governor's plan. New York, a pivotal state in the electoral calculus, stood poised to defy expectations and reshape the narrative of the impending election.

As the conspirators left the clandestine meeting, the echoes of political intrigue reverberated through the corridors of power. New York, a state known for its tumultuous politics, prepared to unleash a seismic shift that would ripple through the nation's electoral landscape. The stage was set for a dramatic confrontation, where personal vendettas intertwined with political destiny.

***

In the heart of Pennsylvania, a political drama unfolded, carefully choreographed to shift the balance of power in the electoral college. The mastermind behind this intricate plan was a coalition of influential figures with allegiances that ran deep within the corridors of political, economic, and cultural power. Their strategy relied on the creation of chaos, uncertainty, and public outcry to manipulate the electoral process.

The first move involved harnessing the power of the press. Pro-John Adams newspapers throughout the state were enlisted to run a series of stories highlighting alleged instances of pro-Adams voters being denied the right to cast their ballots at polling places. The narrative woven was one of injustice, casting doubt on the integrity of the electoral process.

The stories spread like wildfire, igniting a public outcry that echoed through town squares and coffeehouses across the state. Citizens, fueled by a sense of injustice, demanded answers and accountability. The plan had achieved its first objective – creating an atmosphere of uncertainty about the election results in Pennsylvania.

Amidst the tumult, the masterminds behind the scheme discreetly lobbied key legislators sympathetic to their cause. The proposal was clear – pass a law allowing electors representing the state in the electoral college to vote according to their conscience, free from the constraints of the popular vote. The legislators, sensing the public uproar and perhaps swayed by more clandestine motivations, moved swiftly to pass the legislation.

The passage of the new law marked a turning point in Pennsylvania's political landscape. Electors were now unshackled from the obligation to vote by the popular vote, opening the door for strategic manipulation. The next phase involved identifying and approaching electors who could be swayed to cast their votes for John Quincy Adams.

Lobbyists and emissaries worked tirelessly behind the scenes, leveraging a mix of persuasion, promises, and, in some cases, outright bribery. The electors found themselves in a delicate dance of loyalty to the party versus personal conviction. The pressure was immense, the stakes high, and the outcome uncertain.

In parallel, the public outcry continued to crescendo, fueled by the narrative of electoral injustice perpetuated by the orchestrated media campaign. The pressure on electors intensified as the eyes of the nation turned toward Pennsylvania, a state at the epicenter of a political storm.

As the electoral college meeting approached, the masterminds of the plan watched with bated breath. The culmination of their carefully orchestrated strategy hinged on the decisions of individual electors who now held the fate of Pennsylvania's electoral votes in their hands. The stage was set for a grand finale, where the boundaries of political maneuvering blurred, and the outcome would resonate through the annals of American political history.

***

In the dimly lit ambiance of the breakfast nook at the Nashville inn, Andrew Jackson sat across from his campaign manager, his weathered face etched with a mix of weariness and determination. The aroma of coffee hung in the air as they delved into the intricate plan that could reshape the course of the nation's history.

Francis Williamson (leaning in, his voice low) "Mr. President, the time has come to take matters into our own hands. The electoral college, as it stands, might not align with the voice of the people."

Jackson, furrowing his brow, "What do you mean, Francis? I thought we had a solid strategy.

Williamson, sipping his coffee, "The landscape is shifting, sir. We've identified opportunities in key states — New York, Pennsylvania, and Louisiana. If we can control the electors, we can secure your victory."

Jackson, leaning back, contemplative, "Control the electors? I've always believed in the will of the people."

"And we do, sir. But there are forces at play that seek to undermine that will. In New York, they can exploit divisions within the Democratic ranks. The governor there is no friend of Van Buren, and they can use that to their advantage."

"What about Pennsylvania?"

"Pennsylvania is a tinderbox, sir. A media frenzy about voters being denied their rights has created chaos. They already pushed through a change in the law allowing electors to vote their conscience."

Raising an eyebrow, Jackson responded, "Conscience? I thought they were bound by the popular vote?"

"Not anymore, sir. The law has changed. Electors can now vote as they see fit."

Jackson, pausing, "And Louisiana?"

Leaning in, a glint in his eye, Williamson responded, "Louisiana is a different beast. The governor there despises you. He can sway the electors by playing to their disdain for you.

Leaning back in a contemplative gaze, Gen. Jackson said, "This goes against everything I stand for. But if it's the only way to protect the will of the people, we must fight to protect our victory in the popular vote!"

"Sir, we're fighting fire with fire. It's a battle for the soul of this nation. We can't let them manipulate the system."

After a moment of silence, "Do what you must. Protect the people's voice. But remember, we're walking a fine line."

Raising his cup in a toast, Williamson responded, "To victory, Mr. President. The people's voice will prevail."

As the morning cast its glow upon the Tennessee landscape, the die was cast. The plan to protect the Electoral College, a desperate bid to safeguard the people's will, was set in motion. The echoes of this clandestine strategy would reverberate through the pages of history, leaving an indelible mark on the legacy of Andrew Jackson.

Chapter 15

Stop The Steal

December 1, 1828

The grandeur of the Hermitage stood against the Tennessee sky, its sprawling landscape echoing with the whispers of a nation in flux. Inside the mansion, a sense of tranquility veiled the storm that brewed beyond its walls. Jackson, a figure etched in history, found himself in the quiet embrace of his sanctuary when an urgent message arrived by courier, disrupting the calm.

The evening sun cast a warm glow on the House, filtering through the oak trees that stood sentinel around the mansion. Jackson, seated in his study with the weight of responsibility etched on his weathered face, was engrossed in a letter when a servant entered, bearing the urgent missive.

Approaching with a sealed envelope, the servant announced, "Mr. Jackson, a message has arrived from Senator Van Buren. Urgent, sir."

Taking the envelope, his brows furrowed, "What could Martin want at a time like this?"

Breaking the seal, Jackson unfolded the letter and read the terse words that spilled across the paper. His countenance shifted from curiosity to concern.

URGENT! STOP THE STEAL!

ADAMS PLOTTING ELECTORAL COLLEGE SHENANIGANS! HE SEEKS TO USURP THE WILL OF THE PEOPLE!

MARTIN VAN BUREN.

The room seemed to darken as Jackson absorbed the gravity of the message. His peaceful haven now resonated with the urgency that reverberated through the words on the letter. Jackson's mind raced, contemplating the implications of Adams' attempting to manipulate the electoral college – a direct assault on the very essence of democracy.

Rising from his chair, Jackson exclaimed, "Damn him to the depths. Adams won't steal this election under my watch."

Without hesitation, Jackson summoned his advisors and trusted confidants to the study. The air in the room crackled with tension as they gathered around the large oak table, their faces reflecting the gravity of the situation.

Addressing the group Jackson said, "Adams is trying to circumvent the people's will through the electoral college. We won't let him succeed."

Nodding, Francis Williamson responded, "What's our move, General?"

Leaning forward, determination in his eyes, "We'll fight fire with fire. We've identified opportunities in key states. We won't let Adams undermine the voice of the people."

As the night descended on the Hermitage, a strategy took shape. The battle lines were drawn, and the fate of the election hung in the balance. The echo of urgent footsteps, impassioned discussions, and the rustle of papers filled the halls of the mansion.

The quietude of the Hermitage had been disrupted, and in its place emerged the fervor of a leader prepared to defend the principles upon which the nation stood. The stakes were high, and the impending clash in the electoral college would become the crucible in which the destiny of the young republic would be forged.

The moon hung high in the Tennessee night sky. In the wake of the urgent message from Van Buren, Jackson moved with a sense of urgency that echoed through the halls. The oak trees whispered in the evening breeze as Jackson made his way to his office.

The soft lamplight spilled from the windows, revealing Jackson seated at his desk, surrounded by the trappings of leadership. He hastily picked up a quill, its tip scratching across parchment as he penned messages to key figures in his political orbit.

Muttering to himself, "Adams won't get away with this. Not under my watch."

The first message was destined for his campaign's office in Washington City, the strategists entrusted with the intricacies of the election battle.

With a swift motion, Jackson sealed the message with wax, the impression of his personal seal declaring the urgency within. The next message was for Martin Van Buren, the loyal ally who had first sounded the alarm.

MARTIN,

ADAMS' THREAT TO DEMOCRACY MUST BE STOPPED. GATHER IN NASHVILLE IN ONE WEEK OF RECEIPT OF THIS LETTER. ACTION IS REQUIRED.

ANDREW

As the messages piled up, each carrying the weight of urgency, Jackson's mind was a flurry of determination. The meeting at the Nashville Inn would be a gathering of political minds, a strategic conclave to thwart Adams' machinations.

Jackson, handing the messages to a waiting servant, "Send these immediately. Our fight has just begun."

In the days that followed, the messages raced across the country, their contents carrying the urgency of a nation under threat. The Nashville Inn, a quiet bastion in the heart of the city, would soon witness the convergence of political minds prepared to defend the principles upon which the republic stood.

The week passed swiftly, and as the appointed day arrived, the Nashville Inn welcomed the political architects of Jackson's campaign. The air in the inn's meeting room crackled with anticipation as chairs were pulled around a large oak table.

General Jackson, entering the room with a steely gaze, "Adams won't steal this election. We'll fight, and we'll fight hard.

The meeting commenced, a strategic symphony conducted by Jackson, Van Buren, and their trusted advisors. The fate of the electoral college, and with it the soul of American democracy, hung in the balance. In the quiet corners of the inn, the echo of decisive footsteps and hushed discussions reverberated – a prelude to the political storm that was about to be unleashed.

The sun began its ascent over Nashville, casting a warm glow upon the quiet streets. The Nashville Inn stood as a silent witness to the political storm brewing within its walls. The appointed hour had arrived, and the five men who had received Andrew Jackson's urgent messages gathered in a private room for breakfast.

Around the oak table sat men of varied backgrounds, their common thread being unwavering allegiance to the principles of democracy and the man who embodied them – Andrew Jackson. The aroma of fresh coffee mingled with the anticipation that hung in the air.

Martin Van Buren began, "Gentlemen, thank you for answering the call. We find ourselves on the precipice of a constitutional crisis."

Nodding, Francis Williamson chimed in, "Adams is attempting to undermine the very foundation of our democracy. We cannot let this stand."

The gathering comprised not only trusted advisors, but individuals seasoned in the art of politics and law, each contributing a unique perspective to the impending crisis.

Senator Lawrence, whose expertise as a lawyer would be essential in the upcoming fight, leaning in said, 'The Constitution outlines the process, and Adams is trying to circumvent it. We must act within the bounds of the law to expose his machinations."

General Anderson, who served as Jackson's campaign chief military advisor, and served with General Jackson in the war of 1812 chimed in while rubbing his chin, "This is a battle of a different kind, but strategy remains key. If Adams thinks he can manipulate the electoral college, we need to be steps ahead."

Dr. Jefferson, the nation's foremost political theorist and professor at William and Mary College in Virginia, leaned back and said, "Our republic's very fabric is at stake. We must approach this not just as a challenge but as a moment to reaffirm the principles we hold dear."

The room hummed with a shared sense of purpose. They were not just defending a man; they were defending the ideals upon which the nation was founded. The clinking of cutlery and the murmur of other patrons in the inn's dining area became a distant backdrop to the weighty discussions at the table.

Van Buren, sipping his coffee, "Andrew will be down from his room in a minute. He's counting on us to navigate these treacherous waters.

Williamson, leaning forward, "We've identified key states where Adams may attempt to manipulate the electors. Our task is to secure those votes for the people's choice."

Senator Lawrence, nodding, "Legal challenges may be our most potent weapon. If we can expose Adams' maneuvers in court, it could sway public opinion and pressure electors."

General Anderson, tapping a finger on the table, "Timing is crucial. We need to strike before Adams solidifies his plan."

The breakfast table became a war room, where ideas were forged into strategies, and resolve solidified into a plan of action. The fate of the nation rested on their shoulders, and as the morning sunlight streamed through the windows, it illuminated the faces of those determined to defend the democratic principles that had brought them together.

The Nashville Inn cradled the hopes and aspirations of these men as they set forth to confront a crisis that threatened the very essence of the American experiment. The die was cast, and the political stage was set for a showdown that would echo through the annals of history.

As the breakfast meeting continued, the group of men immersed themselves in the intricate web of political strategy. The urgency of the situation demanded a bold and swift response to counter John Quincy Adams' attempts to manipulate the electoral college. It was during this deliberation that a consensus emerged – a public pressure campaign focused on Pennsylvania.

Williamson, "Gentlemen if we're to thwart Adams' plan, we need to act decisively. Pennsylvania holds the key."

Senator Lawrence, "Agreed. The state's electors are crucial in this chess game. If we can keep them true to the people's choice, we disrupt Adams' strategy."

Van Buren, nodding, "as much as I would like to stick it to the governor of New York, I agree. However, how do we ensure that the Pennsylvania legislature stands firm against changing their elector laws?"

General Anderson, leaning forward, "We launch a media campaign, a rallying cry that echoes from Pittsburgh to Philadelphia. Let the people speak out against this attempt to steal their voice."

Dr. Jefferson, "The power of the people has always been a force for change. If we can mobilize

Pennsylvanians to demand their legislators uphold the will of the majority, we send a strong message."

The decision crystallized – a coordinated media campaign to expose Adams' plot and a call to action for the people of Pennsylvania. The group envisioned a campaign that would transcend newspaper headlines, reaching the hearts and minds of citizens across the state.

Williamson, "We'll need the support of pro-Jackson newspapers, influential writers, and public speakers. Let's craft messages that resonate with the common man."

Senator Lawrence, scribbling notes, "Legal arguments will play a role. We'll emphasize the importance of upholding the existing law and the integrity of the democratic process."

General Anderson, leaning back, "We must encourage Pennsylvanians to flood the legislative chambers in Harrisburg. Let them see the strength of public sentiment."

The breakfast table transformed into a command center. Plans were laid out, roles assigned, and the vision of a united front against Adams' machinations took shape.

Van Buren, raising his coffee cup, "To the power of democracy and the resilience of the American people. Let's make history."

As the men toasted to their shared cause, the clinking of cups echoed the gravity of the task ahead. The Nashville Inn harbored the architects of a movement – a movement to safeguard the very principles upon which the nation stood.

In the days that followed, the media campaign unfolded. Pro-Jackson newspapers published scathing exposés, detailing the plot to subvert the will of the people. Flyers were distributed, town halls were organized, and impassioned speeches echoed through the streets. The rallying cry reached every corner of Pennsylvania, and the state began to stir with a fervor that would soon find its way to the steps of the legislative chambers in Harrisburg. The battle for democracy had begun, and the people were ready to make their voices heard.

***

In the streets of Harrisburg, Pennsylvania a buzz of anticipation was in the air as thousands gathered for a protest rally led by pro-Andrew Jackson politicians. The air was thick with both tension and determination. Banners proclaiming, "Protect Our Democracy" and "Respect the Will of the People" waved above the sea of people who had come to defend the integrity of their state's electoral process.

On a makeshift stage, set against the backdrop of the Pennsylvania State Capitol, pro-Jackson politicians took turns addressing the crowd. The cheers and applause of the assembled Pennsylvanians echoed through the city, a testament to their commitment to preserving the democratic principles that stood at the heart of the nation.

State Senator Thompson, raising his voice, "Fellow Pennsylvanians, today we stand united against a threat to our democracy. John Quincy Adams seeks to subvert the will of the people, to silence your voices. We cannot allow this to happen!"

The crowd erupted in cheers, holding signs that declared their allegiance to Andrew Jackson and their determination to resist any attempt to change the rules of the electoral game.

Assemblyman Rodgers passionately exclaimed, "Our state has a proud history, a history of standing up for what is right. We will not be swayed by political maneuvering. Our electoral laws must remain sacrosanct!"

The cheers swelled, resonating through the streets as the people embraced the call to protect the very foundation of their democratic process.

As the rally continued, the pro-Jackson politicians implored the crowd to reach out to their legislators, to flood their offices with letters and visits, urging them to uphold the existing law. The atmosphere was charged with civic duty, a collective commitment to safeguard the democratic rights of every Pennsylvanian.

Senator Thompson, raising his hand for silence, "Today, we send a message to the Pennsylvania Legislature. We, the people, demand that you stand with us, that you stand with the law, and that you reject any attempt to change the rules for political gain!"

The crowd, now a unified force, roared in agreement. The rallying cry echoed off the Capitol's walls, reverberating through the heart of Harrisburg.

Despite the fervor of the protest and the impassioned speeches, the fate of Pennsylvania's electoral laws hung in the balance. As the sun set over Harrisburg, the Pennsylvania Legislature convened to deliberate on the proposed changes to the state's electoral process.

In a sobering turn of events, the legislators voted to amend the law, allowing electors to vote their conscience rather than adhere to the popular vote. The decision sent shockwaves through the crowd, and the cheers that had echoed through the streets turned to gasps of disbelief.

Senator Thompson addressed the crowd, "We may not have won this battle, but the fight for democracy is far from over. We will continue to stand united, to defend the principles that make our nation strong!"

The rally, despite the setback, concluded with a renewed sense of purpose. The people of Pennsylvania, though disappointed, left the Capitol steps with the conviction that their fight for democracy would persist. The echoes of their collective voices lingered in the air, a reminder that the struggle to protect the democratic ideals they held dear would endure.

Chapter 16

The Electoral College

December 17, 1828

Inside the solemn halls of the Pennsylvania State House in Harrisburg, a pivotal moment in American democracy was unfolding. The Electoral College electors, tasked with casting their votes for the President of the United States, had assembled to determine the course of the nation. The weight of their decisions hung in the air, matched only by the gravity of the protests that echoed from the streets outside.

The atmosphere was tense as the electors took their seats in the ornate chamber. The fate of the presidency rested on their shoulders, with the eyes of the nation fixed upon the Commonwealth of Pennsylvania. The room buzzed with subdued conversations and hushed deliberations, each elector wrestling with the responsibility bestowed upon them.

The electors, clad in somber attire, were a group representing various walks of life – farmers, lawyers, businessmen – bound by their duty to participate in this fundamental aspect of the democratic process. The air was thick with anticipation as they prepared to inscribe their choice for the highest office in the land.

Outside the State House, the streets were alive with the clamor of passionate voices. Pro-Jackson and pro-Adams protesters had gathered in distinct clusters, each group vehemently expressing their convictions. Banners waved, slogans were chanted, and the air crackled with tension as the fate of the nation hung in the balance.

A group of Jackson supporters, waving banners adorned with the familiar visage of Old Hickory, shouted slogans demanding the electors honor the will of the people. Across the square, Adams supporters held signs defending the electors' right to vote with conscience, arguing for the principles of independence and individual choice.

Inside the chamber, the electors, aware of the fervor outside, solemnly commenced their duty. The weight of their decision was palpable, as the electors grappled with their commitment to the people and the constitutional mandate to exercise their independent judgment.

Outside, the protests escalated, the voices reaching a crescendo that resonated within the State House. A palpable silence enveloped the room. The eyes of the nation turned toward Pennsylvania, awaiting the pronouncement that would shape the course of history.

The President of the Electoral College, a venerable figure chosen for this significant role, stepped forward to commence the proceedings. The electors from Pennsylvania had gathered to cast their ballots, and at that moment, the destiny of the presidency hung in the balance.

Inside those historic walls. the atmosphere was charged with tension and anticipation. The electors, chosen to represent the will of the people in the Electoral College, had gathered to fulfill their solemn duty. The fate of the presidency hung in the balance, and each elector carried the weight of the nation's expectations.

The diverse group of electors, a microcosm of the state itself, settled into their seats in the grand chamber. Some were vocal supporters of Andrew Jackson, their loyalty rooted in the hero of the Battle of New Orleans. Others ardently stood by John Quincy Adams, championing his intellect, diplomatic acumen, and dedication to public service.

As the President of the Electoral College called the meeting to order, the room echoed with the shuffling of papers and the hushed murmurs of conversation. The debate that ensued was a clash of ideas, principles, and loyalties. Each elector, bound by their conscience and duty, voiced their perspectives with passion and conviction.

Electoral College President, gaveling for order, "Ladies and gentlemen, let us commence the debate. We gather here not merely as representatives of political factions but as stewards of democracy. The floor is open."

The first elector to speak rose from his seat saying, "Fellow electors, I implore you to consider the will of the people. Andrew Jackson embodies the spirit of the common man, and to deny him the presidency is to deny the very essence of our democratic experiment."

A pro-Adams elector responded. Forcefully, "While I respect General Jackson's military achievements, we must prioritize wisdom and experience in these turbulent times. John Quincy Adams possesses the intellect and statesmanship required to lead our great nation."

The debate unfolded, a symphony of competing ideals, as electors passionately articulated their positions. Some argued for Jackson's reputation as a defender of the people, while others emphasized Adams's qualifications and dedication to the principles of governance.

Mr. Davis, a pro-Jackson elector, leaned forward, "Our democracy thrives on the principle of representation. Jackson represents the common folk, those who have long felt overlooked by the political elite. To deny him the presidency is to deny representation to the people we claim to serve."

Mr. Wallace responded, "Representation alone is not enough. Adams brings a wealth of experience, having served as Secretary of State and Ambassador. We need a leader who can navigate the complexities of international relations and ensure the prosperity of our young republic."

The debate ebbed and flowed, echoing through the State House chamber. The exchange of ideas was robust, reflective of the deeply divided nature of American politics in this crucial moment.

Mr. Johnson stood, "My fellow electors, let us not forget the principles that bind us. Democracy demands a fair and conscientious decision. As we cast our votes, let it be in the spirit of preserving the integrity of our democratic process."

The call for unity resonated in the room, reminding the electors of their shared commitment to the democratic ideals that underpinned the nation. The debate had laid bare the profound differences among them, but the moment of decision was quickly coming.

As the President of the Electoral College prepared to call for the vote, the electors took a collective breath, aware that the choices they made would echo through the annals of American history.

The debate among the Pennsylvania electors in the State House reached a fever pitch, echoing with impassioned pleas, principled arguments, and, unfortunately, insinuations of impropriety. As the atmosphere intensified, whispers of alleged attempts to influence votes began to circulate within the chamber.

Mr. Thompson said accusingly, "I've heard whispers, colleagues, of attempts to sway our votes. We must stand firm against any nefarious schemes seeking to undermine the will of the people."

Mr. Reynolds, rising indignantly, "I categorically deny any insinuations of bribery! We are here to uphold the sanctity of our electoral process. Let us not tarnish this solemn duty with baseless accusations!"

The room grew tense as the specter of corruption cast a shadow over the proceedings. Accusations of backroom deals and underhanded tactics added layers of complexity to an already contentious debate.

Mr. Johnson interjected, "Friends, we must proceed with caution. Accusations without evidence only serve to sow discord among us. Let us focus on the task at hand – casting our votes by our principles."

The allegations, though unproven, lingered in the air, threatening to erode the trust among the electors. As the debate continued, some electors couldn't shake the suspicion that unseen forces were at play, attempting to sway the outcome in favor of one candidate over the other.

Mr. Davis pointedly accused, "We must not allow our sacred duty to be compromised. The eyes of the nation are upon us, and we must not falter in the face of potential corruption."

Mr. Wallace defiantly responded, "I find these accusations unfounded and damaging to the democratic process. Let us dispel these rumors and focus on the merits of our candidates."

The debate, now tainted by the shadow of mistrust, pressed on. Each elector grappled with their commitment to the democratic principles they held dear, striving to maintain the integrity of their votes while navigating the tumultuous currents of political intrigue.

As the accusations lingered, the President of the Electoral College, with a stern expression, sought to restore order and guide the electors back to the heart of the matter – the decision that would shape the destiny of the nation. The weight of their duty pressed upon them, urging a resolution that would transcend the divisive currents threatening to pull them asunder.

The moment of decision arrived as the electors prepared to cast their ballots. The air was thick with tension, and the fate of the presidency rested upon the shoulders of these chosen representatives. The debate had been robust, accusations of impropriety lingering, but now the focus shifted to the act that would seal the nation's destiny.

Mr. Thompson rose, "The people of Pennsylvania have spoken through us, and I cast my vote for the hero of New Orleans, Andrew Jackson!"

The proclamation was met with applause from those who had aligned with General Jackson, their conviction resolute. The roll call continued, each elector announcing their allegiance, laying bare the deep divisions that characterized this crucial moment.

Reynolds stood, "I, too, cast my vote with a clear conscience for John Quincy Adams, a leader of wisdom and experience."

The proclamations echoed through the chamber, creating a cadence that mirrored the pulse of a nation watching with bated breath. As the tally progressed, it became evident that the vote hinged on the decisions of the remaining electors.

Mr. Johnson solemnly began to speak, "I approach this decision with the gravity it deserves. My vote is a reflection of my commitment to the democratic principles we hold dear."

The eyes of those assembled fixated on Mr. Johnson, the neutral arbiter in this electoral drama. The weight of the nation's expectations bore down on him as he rose to announce his decision.

Pausing for a moment, Mr. Johnson continued, "In the spirit of compromise and unity, I cast my vote for John Quincy Adams."

The proclamation hung in the air; a moment frozen in time. Gasps and murmurs rippled through the room as the reality of the decision settled upon the gathered electors. The electoral votes of Pennsylvania, a pivotal battleground, had shifted towards Adams.

Mr. Davis, disbelieving, proclaimed, "This cannot be! The people's voice has been silenced."

Mr. Wallace triumphantly said, "Democracy demands compromise, and today, we have chosen a path of unity."

The announcement sent shockwaves through the political landscape. The close vote, with five electors siding with Jackson and the remaining choosing Adams, epitomized the deeply divided nature of the nation. Pennsylvania's decision had tipped the scales, securing the presidency for John Quincy Adams.

As the echoes of the final vote reverberated through the State House, the electors absorbed the gravity of their actions. The democratic process had spoken, but the consequences of this moment would resonate far beyond the confines of the chamber, shaping the course of American history.

***

Martin Van Buren sat in the gallery of the Pennsylvania State House, an impassive observer to the unfolding drama on the floor below. The gravity of the moment weighed heavily on his shoulders as he watched the electors cast their votes, sealing the fate of the presidential election. The division within the Electoral College mirrored the deep rifts that had fractured the nation.

As the last elector's decision was announced, Van Buren absorbed the reality that Andrew Jackson had once again fallen short of the presidency. The cheers and jeers from various corners of the room echoed in his ears, a cacophony of triumph and disappointment.

Leaving the state capital building, Van Buren moved through the bustling streets of Harrisburg with a heavy heart. The weight of the electoral decision pressed upon him, and he knew he had the solemn duty to convey this news to Jackson. The chilly wind swept through the streets, carrying with it the echoes of a political battle lost.

Arriving at his hotel room, Van Buren sat at a wooden desk, the flickering candlelight casting shadows on the walls. He dipped his quill in ink and began composing a letter to the man he had staunchly supported throughout the turbulent campaign.

My Dearest General Jackson,

It is with a heavy heart that I must convey the outcome of the electoral college proceedings in Pennsylvania. The votes have been cast, and the decision is final — John Quincy Adams has secured the presidency.

The dynamics within the electoral college were tumultuous, reflecting the deep divisions that persist in our young nation. The people's voice, while resounding in many quarters, was ultimately overruled by the deliberations of the electors. This election, like the one before it, has proven to be a test of our democratic principles.

You have fought valiantly, and your unwavering commitment to the cause of democracy has inspired many. The road ahead may be challenging, but I know that your dedication to the principles that bind this nation will endure.

I remain at your service, and my support for you is steadfast. Let us navigate this difficult moment with grace and resilience, for the essence of our democratic experiment lies in its ability to weather such storms.

Yours faithfully,

Martin Van Buren

Sealing the letter with wax, Van Buren dispatched a messenger to deliver the missive to Andrew Jackson. The echoes of defeat lingered in the air, but as he gazed out of the window into the night, Van Buren knew that this was not the end. The political landscape may shift, but the enduring spirit of democracy would persist, resilient in the face of trials yet to come.

Chapter 17

A Call For Secession

December 23, 1828

A MESSAGE FROM ANDREW JACKSON

Nashville Register

My Fellow Citizens,

I pen these words with a heavy heart, for they carry the weight of a nation's turmoil and my own profound sorrow. It is with great reluctance that I find myself compelled to address you on a matter of such gravity. I must speak of secession, a topic that should fill any patriot with apprehension and sorrow, yet a course of action that I believe has become a dire necessity.

Our young Republic stands at a crossroads, torn by strife and plagued by political corruption. The foundations upon which our great nation was built are under siege, and the spirit of liberty, so ardently defended by our forefathers, is being eroded.

In the year 1824, I, Andrew Jackson, stood as a candidate for the office of the President of the United States. In a contest marked by the voices of the people, I received the majority of both the popular vote and the electoral college. It should have been a resounding affirmation of our democratic principles, the voice of the people manifesting in their choice for leadership.

However, the circumstances of that election have left a cloud of suspicion and doubt that I can no longer ignore. John Quincy Adams, it is widely believed, secured the presidency through political maneuvering and a so-called "corrupt bargain." This event, a stain on our democracy, cast a shadow of doubt over the legitimacy of the government.

I have wrestled with this issue in my heart, pondered it in my study, and prayed for guidance. The question that looms before us is this: Can we, as patriots, continue to pledge allegiance to a government that has strayed so far from the principles of liberty, fairness, and representation?

My friends, it is with great sadness that I have concluded that we may have no choice but to contemplate secession from the Union. This is not a call to arms or a desire for division; it is a desperate plea to preserve the principles upon which our nation was founded.

It is my fervent hope that this letter serves as a wake-up call, not only to those who share my convictions but to all Americans who believe in the ideals of freedom, justice, and the right to self-determination. The course of action I propose is drastic, but the circumstances in Washington demand nothing less.

We must reflect on our history, on the sacrifices of our forefathers, and on the aspirations that have defined our great nation. We must remember that, in the face of injustice and corruption, the spirit of America has always been one of courage and determination.

Let us, as free citizens, engage in peaceful discourse, debate, and prayer to determine the course of our future. Our collective decision should be grounded in the spirit of democracy, fairness, and love of country.

May we find a path forward, whether through reconciliation or secession, which preserves the principles upon which our Republic was built. May we honor the memory of those who have sacrificed for our liberty and the principles that have guided us since the birth of our great nation.

With respect and a heavy heart,

Andrew Jackson

***

A Call for Southern Resilience

December 23, 1828

In the hallowed pages of the Nashville Register, we find ourselves at a crossroads of history, a juncture where the foundations of our democracy have been shaken to their core. The echoes of the recent electoral college proceedings resonate not only in the halls of power but reverberate across the fields and plantations of the South. It is with a heavy heart and a sense of duty that we, as stewards of the Southern voice, pen these words – a call for resilience and, if necessary, the contemplation of secession.

The events surrounding the 1828 presidential election have left an indelible mark on the tapestry of our young republic. Shenanigans, political machinations, and maneuvers have cast a shadow over the sanctity of the electoral process. While the people's will has been declared in the popular vote, the Electoral College, the supposed guardian of our democratic ideals, has become a stage for backdoor dealings and covert strategies.

The South, a bastion of tradition and principle, cannot stand idly by as the very fabric of our democracy is ripped asunder. The recent election has illuminated a harsh reality – a reality where the machinations of a few can subvert the collective voice of the people. In such dire straits, we are compelled to contemplate the once unthinkable – secession.

The idea of secession is not one to be taken lightly. It is born out of a deep-seated love for the principles that bind us as Southerners, as Americans. It is not an act of rebellion but a declaration of our commitment to the true spirit of democracy – a spirit that refuses to bow to the whims of political maneuvering and partisan ploys.

We must question the legitimacy of a system that allows for such manipulation of the electoral process. The Southern states, with their distinct values and traditions, deserve a platform where their voices are heard, and where their votes are not subject to the caprices of political gamesmanship. If the very institution meant to safeguard our democratic ideals becomes a tool for manipulation, it is our duty to reassess our place within this union.

In calling for resilience, we do not advocate for hasty actions or reactionary measures. Instead, let us engage in a thoughtful discourse about the preservation of our values, the sanctity of our votes, and the future of our Southern way of life. The spirit of the South has weathered storms before, and it is in this spirit that we approach the challenging days ahead.

As we reflect on these tumultuous times, let us remember that the true strength of a nation lies in the resilience of its people. In these pages of the Nashville Register, we pledge to continue the fight for justice, fairness, and the preservation of Southern values. The road ahead may be fraught with uncertainty, but together, united in purpose, we shall navigate these uncharted waters and emerge stronger on the other side.

***

December 28, 1828

The Tennessee State House was a buzz of anticipation as Representative Sampson Henderson, a stalwart figure of rural Middle Tennessee, rose to introduce a resolution that would send shockwaves throughout the Southern states. The atmosphere in the chamber was tense, reflecting the charged emotions that had gripped the region in the aftermath of the recent presidential election.

"Mr. Speaker, esteemed colleagues, and fellow citizens," Henderson began, his voice echoing through the ornate chamber. He was a man of the people, a representative deeply connected to the agrarian roots of Middle Tennessee, and his words carried the weight of the sentiments that echoed across the Southern landscape.

"As we gather in this esteemed hall, we find ourselves at a crossroads in the annals of our great state's history. The recent events surrounding the 1828 presidential election have left us grappling with questions of the sanctity of our democratic process, the honor of our collective voice, and the very fabric of our union."

A hushed silence fell over the assembly as Henderson unfolded the resolution, a document that called for a convention of the Southern states to meet in Nashville at the end of January 1829. The purpose of this gathering was clear — to discuss the viability and necessity of secession from the United States of America. The resolution laid bare the deep-seated frustrations and grievances borne out of the perceived political chicanery of President John Quincy Adams.

"Our beloved South has long stood as a beacon of tradition, resilience, and principled governance. Yet, recent events have cast a pall over our democratic ideals. The Electoral College, meant to safeguard the voice of the people, has become a theater of political maneuvering, a stage where the will of our citizens is subverted by clandestine machinations."

Henderson's words struck a chord with those assembled, and the chamber was filled with murmurs of agreement and understanding. The resolution articulated a sentiment that resonated with the hearts of many Southerners who felt their values and way of life were under threat.

He continued, "Fellow Tennesseans, this resolution is a call to action, a call for us to stand united in defense of our principles. The convention we propose is not a declaration of rebellion but a gathering of statesmen to deliberate on the future of our beloved South. We must ask ourselves whether we can continue within a union where our voices are drowned out by the clamor of political intrigue."

As Henderson concluded his speech, the chamber erupted into applause and cheers from those who supported the resolution. The seeds of secession had been sown, and the resolution would now face the scrutiny of the legislative process. The echoes of Henderson's impassioned words lingered in the air, leaving a profound mark on the course of southern history. The fate of the resolution would be determined in the coming days, as Tennessee and the entire South grappled with the weight of the decisions that lay ahead.

January 1. 1829

The sun dawned upon Nashville, casting a golden hue over the city that seemed to mirror the radiant optimism that had taken root in the hearts of its inhabitants. The day after the historic resolution calling for a convention of the southern states to discuss secession had passed both chambers of the

Tennessee legislature and received the governor's signature, the city found itself bathed in jubilant celebration.

The streets were alive with the rhythmic cadence of triumphant footsteps, and the air vibrated with the harmonious echoes of joyous conversations. Nashville had become a stage for exuberance, a testament to the shared determination of its people to confront the challenges that lay ahead. It was as if the very spirit of the resolution had infused the city with a newfound energy, a collective pulse that resonated through every thoroughfare and alley.

In the town square, a crowd had gathered spontaneously, a diverse assembly that spanned generations, backgrounds, and social classes. There was an air of camaraderie, a sense of unity that transcended the usual divisions. The jubilant spirit was infectious, spreading like wildfire among the citizens who had long felt the weight of political grievances.

Flags fluttered in the breeze, their colors vibrant and defiant, reflecting the pride of a city ready to assert its identity. Musicians, with instruments in hand, played lively tunes that echoed through the square, providing a soundtrack to the jubilation. It was a celebration of Southern resilience, a declaration that Nashville stood at the forefront of a movement destined to shape the course of history.

Local businesses adorned their facades with banners and streamers, their storefronts echoing the sentiments of the resolution. Taverns and inns overflowed with patrons raising toasts to the future, their glasses clinking in unison as if heralding a new era. The jubilant mood spilled over into impromptu gatherings, where friends and neighbors shared laughter and stories, forging connections that transcended the ordinary boundaries of daily life.

At the state capitol, a palpable sense of accomplishment pervaded the corridors. Legislators and officials exchanged congratulatory embraces, recognizing the significance of the resolution they had championed. The governor's signature had given the call for a convention the weight of official endorsement, propelling the city and the state into uncharted territory.

As the sun dipped below the horizon, casting long shadows over the jubilant city, the celebration continued into the night. The glow of lanterns illuminated the faces of those who reveled in the newfound spirit of unity. Nashville, once a mere dot on the map, had become a symbol of Southern determination, a beacon that beckoned the region to gather and deliberate on the path forward.

The jubilant mood of the city of Nashville reverberated far beyond its limits. It was a rallying cry that echoed through the hearts of Southerners across the land, an anthem of resilience that would guide them through the uncertain times that lay ahead.

***

Uniting Voices: Southern States Answer the Call for Secession Convention

January 10. 1829

The Nashville Register

In an unprecedented display of solidarity, the Southern states of Mississippi, Alabama, Florida, Georgia, South Carolina, and North Carolina have unequivocally accepted Tennessee's invitation to a convention in Nashville at the end of January. The purpose of this historic gathering is to deliberate on the prospect of secession from the United States, a response to what many perceive as political shenanigans orchestrated by President John Quincy Adams during the 1828 electoral college vote.

The resolutions of secession passed by these states underscore a growing sentiment among Southerners that their collective voice has been compromised by a series of political maneuvers. The Nashville Register has obtained copies of the resolutions, revealing a shared frustration over what is perceived as the erosion of democratic principles.

Mississippi Leads the Charge

Mississippi, the first state to pass the resolution, expressed its commitment to standing shoulder to shoulder with its Southern brethren in defense of their cherished values. Governor Walter Leake, in a statement to the press, asserted that "the people of Mississippi have spoken through their elected representatives, and we will not stand idly by as our democratic principles are undermined."

Alabama and Florida Echo the Sentiment

Alabama and Florida swiftly followed suit, with both states expressing a commitment to fostering a united front in the face of what they consider political corruption. Governor John Murphy of Alabama emphasized the need for a united Southern response, stating that "we must assess the path forward together, as brothers and sisters in this great Southern family."

Florida Governor William P. Duval echoed this sentiment, emphasizing that the convention would provide a forum for Southern states to deliberate on the most critical issues affecting their future within the Union.

Georgia, South Carolina, and North Carolina Join the Movement

Georgia, South Carolina, and North Carolina joined the chorus of states answering Tennessee's call, each passing resolutions that underscore the need for a collective examination of the challenges posed by the recent electoral college vote. Leaders from these states emphasized the importance of preserving the integrity of Southern representation and securing the region's autonomy within the Union.

As these resolutions are transmitted to Nashville, anticipation is being built for the momentous convention that will bring together representatives from across the Southern states. The eyes of the nation are on this gathering, as the South contemplates its place within the Union and the course of action that will define its future. The Nashville Register will provide extensive coverage of the convention, delivering insights and analysis as events unfold in this critical moment in Southern history.

Chapter 18

The Nashville Convention

January 31, 1828

The day dawned over Nashville with a unique blend of jubilation and pensiveness, an atmosphere that seemed to mirror the collective mood of a city poised on the brink of history. The streets, which had recently echoed with the joyous celebration of the secession resolution passing in the Tennessee legislature, now bore witness to a more contemplative energy.

As Nashvillians traversed the familiar cobblestone paths, their footsteps carried the weight of anticipation and uncertainty. Flags adorned balconies, storefronts, and homes, their colors symbolizing both pride and the gravity of the moment. The jubilant spirit of the recent celebration lingered, but it had now transformed into a more solemn resolve.

In the town square, where revelry had once reigned supreme, a makeshift stage had been erected. A group of musicians tuned their instruments, melodies echoing through the air with a certain solemnity. A diverse crowd gathered, not for unrestrained merriment, but for a communal reflection on the challenges and decisions ahead.

Local leaders, political figures, and citizens from all walks of life assembled their faces painted with a mix of determination and contemplation. The atmosphere was charged with conversations that fluctuated between hope and concern, as Nashvillians grappled with the weight of the decisions to be made at the secession convention.

At a popular tavern near the state capitol, a group of friends gathered for a pre-convention meal. Their laughter, though subdued, conveyed a sense of camaraderie born out of shared purpose. The clinking of glasses was accompanied by discussions about the path the South might take and the repercussions of severing ties with the Union.

The state capitol itself stood as a silent witness to the unfolding drama. Guards patrolled the perimeter, their uniforms a stark reminder of the authority vested in the decisions that would emerge from within those hallowed halls. Banners bearing slogans of Southern unity fluttered in the breeze, providing a backdrop to the gravity of the moment.

Within the capitol, representatives from across the Southern states began to gather. Hushed conversations echoed through the corridors, punctuated by the occasional murmur of agreement or dissent. As delegates from Mississippi, Alabama, Florida, Georgia, South Carolina, and North Carolina arrived, the symbolism of their presence underscored the interconnected fate of the Southern states.

 Sampson Henderson, the architect of Tennessee's resolution, addressed the assembly. His voice, resonant with both determination and humility, conveyed the significance of the occasion. "We stand united, not as separate states, but as a Southern family," he proclaimed, urging the delegates to deliberate with wisdom and foresight.

As the convention officially commenced, a sense of purpose pervaded the air. The eyes of the nation were on Nashville, as this gathering of Southern minds embarked on a journey that would shape the course of history. The jubilant yet pensive atmosphere in the city encapsulated the complexity of emotions that accompanied the Southern states on the eve of their collective destiny.

The cavernous hall within the state capitol echoed with the hushed murmurs of anticipation as the delegates settled into their seats. The air was pregnant with the weight of history, and all eyes turned toward the rostrum, where the Speaker of the Tennessee House of Representatives stood with a gavel in hand.

"Ladies and gentlemen, fellow representatives of our great Southern states, I hereby call this historic convention into session," announced the Speaker, his voice resonating through the hall. A wave of applause and acknowledgment swept across the assembly, acknowledging the gravity of the moment.

He continued, "Before we proceed, let us be mindful of the importance of our deliberations. We gather not merely as representatives of individual states but as stewards of a shared Southern destiny. The decisions made within these walls will shape the future of our region and reverberate across the annals of history."

The Speaker outlined the rules that would govern the proceedings, emphasizing fairness, respect, and the democratic principles upon which the Southern states prided themselves. Delegates were reminded that their duty was not only to their respective constituents but to the collective will of the South.

"As we embark on this journey, let us remember the principles that bind us together: a commitment to liberty, sovereignty, and the preservation of our cherished way of life. This convention is a forum for open dialogue, where the voices of every state shall be heard and respected," proclaimed the Speaker, punctuating his words with the authoritative strike of the gavel.

The agenda was then laid out with meticulous detail. Each item addressed critical aspects of the South's relationship with the Union, ranging from the perceived injustices of recent elections to the preservation of states' rights and the establishment of a framework for collective decision-making.

The Speaker concluded his opening remarks with a call for unity. "Let us approach our deliberations with wisdom, courage, and the understanding that, united, we can forge a path forward that ensures the prosperity and self-determination of our Southern states."

With that, the Southern secession convention was officially in session, and the destiny of the South rested in the hands of those gathered within the hallowed halls of the Tennessee state capitol. The chamber buzzed with a mixture of resolve and expectation as the delegates prepared to navigate the intricate web of decisions that would define their collective future.

As the Speaker, now appointed President of the Convention, concluded his opening remarks, the grand doors of the chamber swung open, heralding the entrance of a figure whose presence commanded the attention of every delegate. The thunderous applause and cheers that erupted as Andrew Jackson strode into the hall echoed off the walls, a testament to the reverence and admiration the delegates held for the man they fondly referred to as "Old Hickory."

Dressed in the characteristic attire that had become synonymous with his public persona—his signature military-style coat and a mop of unruly white hair—the General acknowledged the crowd with a humble nod. As he made his way to the podium, the delegates rose from their seats, a sea of eager faces turning toward the man who had become the rallying point for Southern defiance.

Jackson's progress to the podium was not swift, for at nearly every step, he paused to grasp the outstretched hands of delegates from each state. The chamber resonated with the cacophony of greetings, a chorus of Southern voices expressing gratitude, admiration, and solidarity. The tactile connection with the delegates was a deliberate choice by Jackson, a symbol of his commitment to the shared cause.

Finally reaching the podium, Jackson raised his hand, signaling for the room to settle into silence. The delegates, with bated breath, awaited the words of the man whose leadership had brought them to this pivotal moment in history.

"Esteemed representatives of the Southern states, I stand before you today not as an individual but as a servant of the people, bound by a shared vision of sovereignty and self-determination," began Jackson, his voice carrying the weight of decades of military and political experience.

He delved into the heart of the matter, addressing the grievances that had led them to this juncture. Jackson spoke passionately about the perceived injustices, the erosion of states' rights, and the need for the South to stand united against encroachments on their cherished way of life. His words resonated with a fervor that echoed the sentiments of those gathered.

"As we deliberate on the future of our Southern states, let us remember the sacrifices of those who came before us. The principles of liberty and self-governance are not mere rhetoric but the bedrock upon which our great nation was founded," proclaimed Jackson, his piercing gaze surveying the assembly.

Throughout his address, Jackson struck a delicate balance between statesmanship and a call to arms. His words stirred a deep sense of loyalty and determination among the delegates, instilling in them the conviction that their cause was just and worth fighting for.

As Jackson continued his address, the chamber erupted once more in resounding applause. Delegates rose to their feet, their fervor a visible manifestation of the unity and purpose that had coalesced within the Southern secession convention. Jackson stepped away from the podium, leaving a charged atmosphere, pregnant with the weight of decisions yet to be made. The fate of the South hung in the balance, and the delegates were now tasked with shaping its destiny.

Amidst the charged atmosphere, Andrew Jackson's voice cut through the tension, resonating with a resonance that mirrored the fervor of the Southern delegates. His speech became a rallying cry, each word a call to action that echoed the sentiments of the aggrieved states assembled in Nashville.

"Brothers and sisters of the South," Jackson continued, his voice strong and unwavering, "we stand at a crossroads, where the path of self-determination diverges from the dictates of a distant and overreaching government. Our ancestors fought for a vision of freedom, a vision where each state could govern itself, charting its course without interference."

With each carefully chosen word, Jackson laid bare the grievances that had fueled the flames of secession. He spoke of the perceived injustice in the halls of power, the erosion of the principles upon which the nation was built, and the betrayal that had unfolded in the 1828 election.

"As I stand before you, I see not just representatives of states, but guardians of liberty. We are united by a common cause—a cause that transcends party lines and state borders. We are bound by the belief that our destiny is our own to forge," proclaimed Jackson, his eyes surveying the faces of the delegates.

The speech was punctuated by interruptions, not of dissent, but of overwhelming support. Standing ovations rippled through the convention hall as Jackson spoke to the hearts of those who felt the weight of the perceived injustices. The echoes of applause reverberated off the walls, a testament to the unity that had been forged in the crucible of shared grievances.

"And so, my fellow Southerners, the time has come for us to assert our rights, to declare our independence from a government that has lost sight of the principles that once bound us together. The corrupt bargain that denied us our voice will not go unanswered," declared Jackson, his voice rising with a resolute determination.

The delegates, moved by Jackson's words, responded with cheers that shook the very foundations of the convention hall. The applause swelled; a tidal wave of affirmation cascaded over the assembly. In that moment, Andrew Jackson stood not just as a political figure but as a symbol of Southern defiance, a torchbearer for those who sought to reclaim what they perceived as their birthright.

As the standing ovation subsided, Jackson took a step back from the podium, his gaze fixed on the multitude of faces before him. The gravity of the decision ahead hung palpably in the air, and the delegates, united by a shared vision, looked to one another with a newfound determination. The course of Southern destiny had been set in motion, and the fervor ignited by Jackson's impassioned speech would be the guiding flame in the turbulent days to come.

The chamber buzzed with fervent discussions, impassioned pleas, and heated arguments as delegates from each Southern state articulated their stances on the pivotal question of secession. The appointed committee, composed of distinguished members, withdrew to a side room to deliberate and craft a document that would articulate the grievances of the Southern states and declare their intent to break away from the Union.

On the convention floor, each speaker addressed the assembly with conviction, embodying the sentiments of their respective constituencies. Some argued that secession was the only path to preserve the principles of liberty and self-governance, echoing Jackson's sentiments. Others, cautious and measured, urged patience and diplomacy, emphasizing the potential consequences of such a drastic step.

Delegate after delegate took the podium, weaving together historical precedents, constitutional interpretations, and heartfelt appeals to the crowd. The debates were punctuated by moments of tension, with tempers flaring and emotions running high. The chamber became an arena where the future of the South hung in the balance.

As the days unfolded, the committee diligently worked on the declaration of secession, laboring over each phrase to ensure it encapsulated the collective grievances of the Southern states. The task was not merely drafting a document; it was an endeavor to immortalize the spirit of rebellion against perceived tyranny.

Within the convention hall, the atmosphere oscillated between anticipation and trepidation. Delegates engaged in fervent discussions during recesses, seeking common ground and contemplating the weighty decision they were about to make. The fate of the Southern states rested in the hands of those gathered in Nashville, and the deliberations were fraught with the gravity of the moment.

Finally, after three days of impassioned debates and meticulous drafting, the committee presented the

Declaration of Secession to the Assembly. The document spoke of usurpations, infringements on states' rights, and a government unresponsive to the concerns of the Southern states. The ink on the parchment bore witness to the culmination of grievances that had simmered for years.

The solemn atmosphere in the convention hall intensified as the spokesperson for the committee, a distinguished delegate with a resonant voice, began to read aloud the Declaration of Secession. Each carefully chosen word echoed through the chamber, punctuating the charged air. The gravity of the moment was palpable, and the eyes of every delegate were fixed on the speaker.

"Assembled delegates," the spokesperson began, "we, the representatives of the Southern states, stand before you to present a declaration that encapsulates the shared sentiments of our constituents, the grievances that have festered unaddressed, and the principles that guide our path forward."

The declaration outlined a litany of perceived injustices, citing alleged usurpations of states' rights, disregard for the Constitution, and the erosion of the principles upon which the Union was founded. It concluded with a resolute assertion of the Southern states' inherent right to dissolve their political connection with the United States.

Debate ensued, and the convention floor became a forum for impassioned discourse. Delegates rose to express their unwavering support for the declaration, emphasizing the imperative of defending Southern liberties and preserving the legacy of self-governance. Others voiced reservations, urging caution and exploring alternatives to secession.

One delegate, a seasoned statesman from Georgia, spoke with measured eloquence, cautioning against the irreversibility of such a monumental decision. "While our grievances are real and profound," he argued, "we must consider the consequences of severing ties with the Union. Is secession the only recourse available to us, or can we still seek redress within the framework of the Constitution?"

Another delegate, fervently waving a copy of the declaration, countered with fiery rhetoric. "Our rights have been trampled upon for far too long! The time for negotiation has passed. We must reclaim our sovereignty and forge a new path for the South."

The hall echoed with a cacophony of opinions, ranging from calls for immediate secession to pleas for further deliberation. Emotions ran high, reflecting the gravity of the decision at hand. The delegates grappled with the weight of history, knowing that their votes would shape the destiny of the Southern states.

As the debate unfolded, alliances were formed, compromises were suggested, and impassioned pleas were made. The atmosphere remained charged with tension, and the fate of the Southern states hung in the balance. The Declaration of Secession, a document that would echo through the annals of history, awaited the collective decision of those assembled in the convention hall.

The tension in the convention hall reached its zenith as the roll call for the vote on the declaration began. Each delegate, with a sense of gravity in their step, approached the voting booth to cast their ballot. The murmurs of conversation gradually subsided, replaced by the rhythmic cadence of names being called.

"Delegate Abernathy?"

"Aye."

"Delegate Baldwin?"

"Nay."

The echoes of each vote reverberated through the hall, signaling the irreversible decision facing the Southern states. Delegates, with conviction etched across their faces, cast their ballots, fully aware that the outcome would shape the destiny of their region.

As the final votes were tallied, the president of the convention, a seasoned statesman with a weathered countenance, stood to address the assembly. His voice carried a mix of solemnity and determination as he announced the result.

"By a vote of thirty-five ayes to eleven nays, the Declaration of Secession is hereby adopted. The Southern states of Tennessee, Mississippi, Alabama, Florida, South Carolina, and North Carolina are solemnly seceded from the United States and are henceforth their own nation."

The words hung in the air, heavy with historical significance. A mixture of emotions swept through the convention hall – jubilation, solemnity, trepidation. Some delegates exchanged triumphant glances, while others bowed their heads in contemplation.

The president of the convention, with a firm yet somber expression, raised the gavel and brought it down decisively, marking the end of the secession convention. The sound echoed through the hall, symbolizing the finality of a decision that would reshape the course of American history.

Outside the convention hall, the news of secession spread rapidly through the jubilant, yet apprehensive crowd gathered in Nashville. Cheers of triumph mingled with the weight of uncertainty, as the Southern states embarked on a path that diverged from the Union.

The delegates, having concluded their historic deliberations, dispersed from the convention hall, each carrying the weight of their role in a momentous decision. The Southern states, having cast their votes, now stood at the threshold of a new chapter – one marked by independence, resilience, and the challenges of forging a nation born from the crucible of secession.

Epilogue

Louisiana Declares Independence, Formation of République of Louisiana Announced

Louisiana Advertiser

January 31, 1829

Baton Rouge, Louisiana—In a historic and unprecedented move, the Louisiana Legislature has passed articles of secession, officially breaking away from the United States and forming a new sovereign nation known as the République of Louisiana. This bold declaration comes amidst ongoing discussions among other Southern states in Nashville, where they are considering a joint secession.

The articles of secession passed with overwhelming support in both chambers of the Louisiana Legislature, asserting the state's right to self-determination and independence. The newly established République of Louisiana boldly claims the entirety of the Louisiana Purchase territory as its rightful domain, a sweeping assertion that dramatically reshapes the political landscape of the American South.

Governor Jean-Baptiste Leclerc, a fervent advocate for secession, addressed the legislature and the public in a stirring speech, proclaiming the birth of the new nation. "Today, we stand as a free and sovereign people, no longer bound by the unjust and corrupt practices of a distant and indifferent government," he declared. "The République of Louisiana shall rise as a beacon of liberty and justice, encompassing the vast and fertile lands of all the Louisiana territories. Our destiny is now in our hands."

The move by Louisiana has sent shockwaves through the country, particularly as the other Southern states convene in Nashville to deliberate their collective response to perceived injustices by the federal government under President John Quincy Adams.

The secession of Louisiana marks a significant escalation in the growing tension between the Southern states and the federal government, raising questions about the future of the Union.

Senator Philippe Duval, a key architect of the secession articles, expressed confidence in the viability and prosperity of the new nation. "The vast resources and strategic position of our territory ensure that the République of Louisiana will thrive independently. We invite our Southern neighbors to recognize our sovereignty and consider similar actions to safeguard their interests."

The articles of secession outline a framework for governance, emphasizing principles of self-governance, economic independence, and the protection of individual liberties. The new nation aims to establish a robust agricultural economy, leveraging the fertile lands of all of Louisiana to ensure prosperity and stability.

Reactions from other states and political leaders have been mixed. Some Southern states have expressed solidarity and admiration for Louisiana's decisive action, while Northern states and federal officials have condemned the move as illegal and unconstitutional.

As the République of Louisiana takes its first steps on the international stage, the nation watches closely, contemplating the implications of this dramatic shift. The coming days and weeks will undoubtedly bring further developments as Louisiana charts its course as an independent nation and other states weigh their paths in this tumultuous period of American history.

The Louisiana Advertiser will continue to provide comprehensive coverage of this unfolding story, bringing you the latest updates and analysis as the situation evolves.

AUTHOR'S NOTE

I can promise you, the reader, that this project didn't start as an indictment of the 2024 (release year) Presidential Election or the candidates in it. Because of the similarities between the 1828 election, which was a rematch between the candidates in the 1824 Presidential Elections, John Quincy Adams and Andrew Jackson, and the similarities in candidates and people's reactions to those candidates, leaning into the indictment of the modern election seemed natural and omnipresent.

The idea for this alternate history arose from President Donald Trump's off-the-cuff remark while in office. He remarked, "If Andrew Jackson were President during the Civil War, he would have ended it quickly." As an avid amateur Civil War historian (that is a fancy way of saying history nerd), I thought to myself "If Andrew Jackson were President during the Civil War, he would be dead, because he was already old when he was President to begin with. However, if there was a Civil War during Andrew Jackson's time as President, he would probably have been leading the rebellion because that meant that Adams electioneered the 1828 election like he was accused of doing in the 1824 election." Hence, the idea for this book was born. After fleshing out the idea with my brother (the sci-fi nerd of the family) creating the alternate universe that I hope to develop in future novels and conducting research into the 1828 election, this book is the product of all that work. I hope you enjoy the read.

OTHER BOOKS BY THE AUTHOR

Unknown Soldier: World War 1

ABOUT THE AUTHOR

David Preston is a lifelong avid reader and student of History. He studied Political Science at the University of South Alabama. David is a recovering politician, reporter, and current business owner. He was born in Gurden, Arkansas, and has lived in Plano, Texas, and Hernando, Mississippi. He currently resides in Mobile, Alabama where he has lived for 30 years.

9 798990 562240